BOX

GIRL

BOX

SARAH WITHROW

GIRL

A GROUNDWOOD BOOK

DOUGLAS & McINTYRE   TORONTO   VANCOUVER   BUFFALO

Groundwood Books/Douglas & McIntyre
720 Bathurst Street, Suite 500
Toronto, Ontario M5S 2R4

Distributed in the USA by Publishers Group West
1700 Fourth Street
Berkeley, CA 94710

We acknowledge the support of the Canada Council for the Arts,
the Ontario Arts Council and the Government of Canada through
the Book Publishing Industry Development Program for our
publishing activities.

ONTARIO ARTS COUNCIL
CONSEIL DES ARTS DE L'ONTARIO

National Library of Canada Cataloguing in Publication Data

Withrow, Sarah, 1966-
Box girl
A Groundwood book.
ISBN 0-88899-407-9 (bound) ISBN 0-88899-436-2 (pbk.)
I. Title.
PS8595.I8455B69 2001   jC813'.54   C2001-930216-9
PZ7.W57Bo 2001

Cover illustration by Janet Wilson
Design by Michael Solomon
Printed and bound in Canada

To Janet Knights,
from whom I stole Clara's smile.

SHE'S THERE. IT'S COLD AND THE DEW HAS
seeped through the toe of my left sneaker. I can feel the heat
of the rising sun on the back of my head.

She's maybe twenty feet away, sitting on the bench near
the rock pile in the center of Skeleton Park. I open my mouth
to call out but change my mind.

I should go.

I take a step. A stick cracks under my foot. I stop to see
if she'll turn around. No. I keep going, holding my breath.
I move beyond the shade of the tall trees and let the dawn
warm my whole body. Almost there. My heart jumps and I
can't stop my feet from running the rest of the way. I reach
for her shoulder, but the second before I touch her she turns
toward me. Her moon face catches the morning glow. Her
eyes are big and full.

I lie down on the bench beside her and tuck my head in
her lap. I feel my mother's fingers first against my temple,
then running through my hair. I'm all warm.

❧

7

I open my eyes to look at her and instead see a flash of light glinting off the streetlight onto my sleepy face.

When she's here and she touches me, those are the best dreams.

I turn my head into my pillow to try to bring her back. But she has disappeared and the best I can imagine is an empty bench.

CHAPTER ONE

I'M SITTING ON THE FLOOR IN FRONT OF the mirror on my closet door.

School starts tomorrow. I know those guys think that I'm dying to step into Anisha's platform shoes and rule the school. She moved to Ottawa and, as her ex-best friend, they naturally think I'm next in line to the throne. What they don't know is exactly how *ex* I am.

They can find someone else for Anisha's job, because I've got other plans. Traveling plans. My new life in France will be clean of everything that came before. I'm going to be a loner until Mom sends for me. It won't be long. Any day now Dad will get the call, and I'll be flying away from here forever.

I reach up into the closet and pull on a pair of white pants that are short on me. I throw them onto the bed behind me with the six other rejected outfits.

The hardest part about deciding to be a loner is creating a good loner outfit. I want to look like one of those rebel girls in the movies who is secretly more beautiful than the pretty girls.

Anisha was pretty. She had perfectly smooth skin, like dark honey, and long, glistening black hair. I bowed down to her like she was the Queen of Sheba. I gave her my black cat T-shirt just because she said she liked it. And I let her trade me on the nail polishes we got from the dollar store because she said the red I got went better with her complexion than the orange she bought.

I was her lady-in-waiting. I was one of those dolls that isn't Barbie but is made to stand beside her at parties − one of those cheap imitation Barbies whose legs won't bend.

I part my hair down the middle and comb it straight against my ears. It makes my head pointy. My eyebrows arch up way too high on my forehead so that I always seem surprised, but my face isn't so bad that it's ugly. I have my mother's deep-set, spooky charcoal gray eyes at least, even if my hair is stringy and mousy. Leon says it's golden. Dad says it's like light, light, light chocolate.

I run my fingers through it to fluff it up.

I should show up like this, in my undershirt with my hair mussed.

"Leave me alone." I mouth the words a couple of times and toss my head.

I try to think of real loners and come up with J.W. Reane, the guy who spits on his arm and then draws pictures in the spit. He talks to the ceiling when he answers in class, like he's talking to some fly up there. Even the teachers don't like calling on him.

I go to my desk for the postcards. They're in a big envelope at the back of the top drawer. I toss the clothes off the bed and arrange the cards under the comforter in case Dad comes in. I listen for sounds in the hall and start the spell. I touch the sides of each postcard in order.

"North, East, South, West. Who is the one that you love the best?"

I whisper the chant. If I do it wrong on one of the postcards, I start over again. That's one of the rules.

RULES FOR THE SPELL

1. Don't tell anyone about the postcards. If anyone knows, it will break the spell.

2. Touch every side of every postcard in order every night. Chant while touching each side. If the spell is interrupted, start over again from the beginning. Contact with

source cannot be secured unless the spell has been properly completed.

3. Build the box immediately after chanting while the cards still have energy in them. The first postcard is the floor and cards 2 to 5 are the walls. The writing sides must face in. Lean them against each other to make them stand up. No glue, paper clips, staples, gum or bending the cards is allowed.

4. The box has to stand up for at least one minute in order to secure contact with source.

It's hard to make the box on the bed because the mattress can shift and knock the whole thing down. But I can't do it on the desk anymore since Dad walked in that time and almost caught me.

It was 2:07 A.M. I told him I was writing a post-card to Anisha.

The desk top was slippery for the cards. The sheet on the bed gives them traction and it makes less noise when the cards fall down. The box is never perfectly square because the postcards aren't all the same size. The floor usually ends up floating in the middle, only touching one or two of the wall cards. I try not to let the gaps at the side and the bottom be too big, so my chant energy won't leak out.

Some nights it takes a long time to make the box, and I have to start over from the beginning.

When the box is standing, I put myself inside it. I close my eyes and make myself be in the box. I concentrate on the writing on the walls. My head follows her hand drawing the letters, the loops, the arcs, the crosses on the t's, the dots above the i's. I always end with the loop on the l in the word *Angel*. It's my goodnight word.

CHAPTER TWO

FIRST DAY OF GRADE EIGHT. I'M BEHIND the willow tree in the McBurney schoolyard. Marcia Whittaker's in the yard and I can tell she's looking for me.

Anisha hated Marcia. When she saw Marcia coming down the hall, she would turn her back to her.

I don't hate Marcia, exactly. She's always flipping her shoulder-length fake-orange hair so that you want to chop it off, and she wears too much make-up, and tops so short that you can see her skinny ribs sticking out – but I don't hate her.

I watch her find Tim. She walks over to him and they start talking but they are both looking over each other's shoulders for someone more popular. They talk for a while and then they seem to give up pretending to be interested in one another.

I'm chuckling under my breath when someone taps me on the shoulder. I turn with a start.

"Sorry, didn't mean to scare you," she says. The girl's thick glasses magnify her large brown eyes. Also, she's got a gap between her two front teeth, which I can't help noticing because she's smiling like a rabid dog. I've seen her around the neighborhood. I thought she went to Central.

"What's so funny?" she says, smiling, like she's ready to get the joke, whatever it is.

"What?" I say. She's got on knee-length navy blue shorts and one of those striped T-shirts that looks permanently wrinkled. Her boobs are big enough that the shirt tents up between them. She looks like she walked out of a funhouse mirror — one that makes her top half seem squashed and her legs all gangly. She's a bit chub round the middle and her arms look short, or maybe they look that way because her legs are long. Her black hair is plastered to her high forehead with bobby pins, as if it's a toupee and might fly off.

"I heard you laugh. What's so funny?" she asks again.

"Nothing. I wasn't laughing at anything." I start walking toward the school. She keeps pace beside me.

"I'm Clara," she says, holding out her hand for me to shake.

"Gwen," I say, but leave her hand hanging. She

15

laughs and slaps her leg. The sound cracks the morning air. Marcia is watching us.

"You mean, like Gwendoline?" Clara says.

"Yeah. I don't see what's so hilarious about it." I'm ready to walk away but then Clara puts her hand on my shoulder. I want to squirm away from it and run.

"I wasn't laughing at you, my dear. I was laughing with you. How too bad for you to be stuck with that. You should have been called Isabel."

"Why should I be called Isabel?"

"Why not?" she says, shrugging. The long arms of the willow bend in the wind behind her. I imagine them dusting off the spot on my shoulder where she touched me, wiping me clean.

"You can't call a person anything you want. A person has the name that he or she has and that person is stuck with that name. There are rules in life." I move off.

"Isabel," she calls after me. I stop, aggravated by the sound of my new name. She catches up to me, grinning like an overgrown hyper kid who's tricked someone into eating a bug.

"I prefer to be called by my correct name. It's Gwen, not Isabel. Why would you think to call me that? You don't know me."

"Because it's beautiful. Isabella. It's-a-beautiful," she says in an Italian accent and moves her arms wide apart like she means the whole world, like she thinks the whole world is-a-beautiful. "It's way better than Gwendoline." The soft edges of her voice tickle my ears like feathers. A strand of too-long bang has worked its way free from a bobby pin and is blowing against her wide nose.

"I'm Gwen, okay? Just plain Gwen," I say. I lift my eyes to the sky like J.W. Reane, and walk away in time to avoid Marcia. Maybe those two will make friends.

Marcia passes Clara who's looking at me, laughing like I said something funny.

I wander the halls, pretending to search for my classroom. Like I wouldn't know exactly where it was after eight years at McBurney. I looked up to the grade eights when I was little. I still remember Mom picking me up at lunch time in grade three, and me whining all the way home because I wanted to eat in the lunch room with my friends.

What a brat I was.

The halls are bare without little-kid art on them. Pretty soon Mr. Kurtzman will have his grade ones busy doing Black Magic crayon drawings and construction-paper leaves. Maybe I'll be in Paris by then.

I turn a corner and Tony's coming down the hall toward me. He stops short.

"Oh. Hey," he says. He's grown. Anisha told me

that he was going to Toronto this summer to work at his brother's corn-dog booth at the Exhibition.

"Hey," I say and walk on by.

Anisha thought Tony was so hot when he started here last year. He grew up in Toronto, but his parents decided to move because his cousin got arrested for dealing drugs and they didn't want Tony getting into that. It used to be Anisha had a thing for Nick Kotopoulis, but his family switched him to a private school because he scored high on an IQ test. I don't know who Anisha would have gone for if Tony hadn't shown up. She went on and on about his hands and his hair. "His hair is so soft and springy, like those little curls would stay in even if he had just taken off, I don't know, like, a motorcycle helmet," she said. I had to listen to stuff like that all the time.

The bell rings.

Marcia is not in my class. That's something, at least. I'm so relieved that I smile at Clara, the new girl, when she chooses a seat beside me. Except then she also chooses the stall next to me in the washroom when we're changing for gym. We're supposed to get a new gym this year — one with change rooms so we won't freeze walking down the hall in our shorts. I'm glad we don't have a change room now so that I don't have to watch Clara watch me undress. I change slowly on purpose so that Clara will finish first and leave, but after I hear her door open, I look under my door and see her feet outside my stall. When I come out, she's standing against the wall smiling at me. I try to avoid her eyes.

Later, I take my time getting to the art room so that Clara will be sitting down by the time I get there. Instead, she's waiting by the bulletin board outside the room. She follows me in and sits down beside me. I raise my hand and ask to go to the washroom.

I have to keep my life clean and uncomplicated so that I'm ready to pick up and go to France at a moment's notice. That means absolutely no friends.

Everyone turns to look at me when I get back to the studio. Ms. Lenore is droning on about what an exciting year it's going to be. I take an empty seat at the back.

And then it happens. Clara gets up – while Ms. Lenore is talking – walks over and sits beside me. I watch Ms. Lenore follow her with her eyes, but she doesn't stop talking.

When we go back to our classroom, Clara sits beside me again. She leans over and says, "You're shy, aren't you?" I give her the dirtiest look I can muster and she gives me one back. Her narrowed eyes are laughing at me.

I see Tim look at Clara and whisper something to Tony and then they both break up. Knowing Tim, it was some snide remark about her chest. Clara gives them this real sarcastic look. At least she's not stupid. She moves her head around a lot, like she thinks there's tons of action going on and she doesn't want to miss any of it. Makes her look like a chicken.

I take my lunch outside so that she can't sit beside me in the lunch room. I make plans for France. I mentally pack my bags. I want to take one of the portraits of me and Dad. That will need special packing. I thought about taking the one of the three of us, but I don't know how Mom would be about that. I mentally stuff one of the smaller portraits into Dad's green duffel bag, but it's not wide enough so I mentally tie it to the bottom of Leon's big purple knapsack. I can mail it back to him once I get there.

The clothes don't matter, because I don't know what's in fashion in France. I'll need new clothes. If Mom doesn't have the money for them, I'll get a job. I'll get a paper route and become fluent in French by reading the paper, watching TV and listening to the radio. I will read the paper on the balcony off my bedroom overlooking the Seine. I will have a small table beside me where I will rest my bottled water, cheese and baguette. I will go out there in the morning to eat strawberries for breakfast out of a blue bowl. I will lean out over the river and Mom will call to me to be careful and I will call back to her that I am trying to feel the sun on my cheek.

I'm waving to my daydream French neighbors when the bell rings.

I'm ready to be completely rude to Clara the second she opens her mouth, but she doesn't say anything. Every time I look over at her, she turns her head and smiles.

They let us out at two o'clock. I stall, organizing some stuff in my desk. Clara waits. When I lift my head, she pats her desktop like it's a lost friend.

"It's the tiniest room in existence," she says. I stare at her and the classroom fades. The postcard walls of my spell box snap up around me like Pop-Tarts. Instantly, I am transported into my tiniest room. I touch the indents of the pen-pressed walls with my mind's fingers.

"Hello? Isabella. Where'd you go?" Clara's waving her hand in front of my face. The box room collapses and I land at my desk in Room 13 at McBurney Public School. I stand up and gather my empty binder, pens and owl-head eraser.

"The tiniest room in existence," I repeat to cover. "Or a ballroom for ants if you leave your lunch in there too long." I can hear her fake laugh

21

echoing behind me as I run down the hall to the main exit.

At least she doesn't try to walk with me on the way home. Lucky me, we go the same way. I pretend I don't notice she's behind me. I keep waiting for her to try to catch up, but she leaves me alone except when she turns off at Raglan. Then she yells, "Bye, just plain Gwendoline Isabella. See you tomorrow," like she thought we were walking together. She must live somewhere in the Fruit Belt, where the streets have names like Cherry and Plum and you can never figure out which way you're going because the roads go diagonal and around and stuff. I've twice gotten lost up there looking for Division Street.

I don't know what to do when she waves at me. I wave back.

That's all she's getting out of me, though. We are not going to be friends.

CHAPTER THREE

WHEN I GET HOME I HEAR THE TV upstairs. It's too early for Dad to be home. Leon must be over watching a ball game. He says he'd watch too much television if he had cable at his place, so instead he's over here all the time watching TSN. I go up and flop on the beanbag chair beside him.

"Hey, how was your first day at school? Any cute new guys?" he says, waggling his eyebrows. Leon thinks he's so hip. He wears his keys on a chain that hangs from his belt loop to his pocket. How stupid is that?

"No. It's the same old crowd, except Anisha's gone."

"And?"

"And there is one new girl who thinks I'm going to be her best friend because she sits beside me in class." Leon shakes some peanuts into his mouth straight from the bag.

"That's the worst. Last thing you need is someone cramping your style in your last year at McBurney."

"Exactly," I say, sitting up and taking the peanuts from him. "I mean, it's not like she's so, so terrible. She talks weird. She's big, not fat, but she has little arms, and she moves her head like a chicken."

"Don't want to be seen with her then."

"Shut up. That's not what I mean. She's really strange. She doesn't know me and she keeps following me around and keeps sitting beside me. I mean, what is that?"

Leon shrugs.

"Sounds like she's the new girl and she wants to make friends."

"But why me?"

"Well, it's like you said. She doesn't know you. Maybe she's mistaken you for someone who is perfectly charming instead of seeing you for the true ogre you are." He turns his square head my way and grins with peanut husks all over his teeth.

"You're disgusting, Melon." Melon is what I call Leon when he's being a thick-headed goof, which is most of the time. "You're sitting in my beanbag chair."

"So, you have a seat."

"But I had that chair worked in perfectly and

you're ruining it with your enormous bum and you're getting peanuts all over it. Give me the remote. I want to watch a movie." I reach for it and he shoves me away. I can smell the peanuts on his breath as I wrestle for it.

"Get off me. I was here first. Don't you have homework?"

"You don't get homework the first day. Don't you have a job?"

"I'm working at home today."

"No, you're not. You're sitting in my beanbag chair watching my TV in my house when you're supposed to be working. And Dad isn't here. You shouldn't be here." He turns his head from the TV, with his face scrunched up.

"I hate it when you get like this. I used your pen, too. I hope that's all right. And the phone, and I touched the doorknob when I came in. I didn't know I needed your permission. I wish you would make some new friends. You've been so uptight since Anisha left. It's a beautiful day out. You shouldn't be watching TV."

"Oh, so it's fine for you to do it, but I should be out in the park begging for new friends?" I stomp out and catch my mad face in the ghost room mirror on my way down the hall. That door should be left shut, I think, pulling it closed.

"I didn't mean that," he calls after me. I continue my stomp down the hall and slam my own door to make the house shake.

>‑

On the front of the first postcard is a photograph of a family camping by a river. You can tell from the mother's beehive hairdo and the father's black-rimmed glasses that the camping trip took place some time in the 1950s. There are two kids in the picture, a boy and a girl. And a dog. Everyone is smiling. Even the dog. This postcard came from France three weeks before my thirteenth birthday last April.

Dear Gwen,

I think about you all the time. I miss you.

Love Mom

There's a lot of white space between the last sentence and where it's signed. Like she couldn't think of anything more to put.

I pulled it out of the mailbox, saw the handwriting and my name and, before I read it, I felt like someone was stomping on my chest. I hid it behind the top drawer of my desk. I didn't tell anyone about it. I felt like it might blink out of existence if I told anyone. I waited for the house to be empty before I took it out to read it again.

I read it every day. And I spent the rest of that

month running home from school to see if another card had come.

Waiting like that – at first I was so happy. I thought it was the beginning of something. I felt like I could hold my breath until something – anything – happened. It felt that close to being real.

But nothing happened.

"North, South, East, West. Who is the one that you love the best." I go through the chanting twice to make a postcard come tomorrow. I sit in the spell box with my hands over my closed eyes and reach for her. I picture a new postcard waiting for me under the darkness of a magician's cloak. When I open the mailbox tomorrow, that's where the postcard will travel from, out of the magic darkness along a silver thread of light.

CHAPTER FOUR

I PUT ON A BLUE T-SHIRT THAT SAYS, "MY parents went to Barbados and all they brought back was this lousy T-shirt." This will scare Marcia.

Then, to make sure, I pull my hair into a tight ponytail that comes out the middle of the top of my head. What a total idiot. If you were in a different country and didn't know what was supposed to be cool, you might think I looked good. With my eyebrows that arch way too far up, I could easily be from someplace else...like Mars.

I expect Dad to say something but he just gives the ponytail a little yank.

"Ow."

"I'm sorry, Princess."

"Dad. I told you not to call me that."

I sit down, eat my peanut butter on toast and think about how not like a princess I am. Dad hands me a white envelope and I almost choke on a crust. My mind is racing. Maybe something came in the mail yesterday after all. Maybe Leon got it out to show Dad. I'll kill him.

There's no writing on it. He shoves it at me.

"Take it. My arm's getting tired," he says.

I open it slowly. It's a card with a sketch of me dressed like a superhero with a huge "G" on the front of my shirt. I can tell from the style of the sketch that Leon did it. He made me really hot, too – tall and curvy with big bulging muscles.

Inside is the word "Sorry" written in Leon's handwriting. I take a deep breath and hold it.

"Yeah, like I look like that," I say to Dad and throw the thing on the table. What a Melon. It's like he thinks I'm his adopted niece or something and he's failing his uncle test. I almost like him when he isn't trying to make me like him.

"I thought it was a nice card," Dad says.

"Yeah, you're right. Tell Leon that I liked it, okay? Tell him I like it that he gave me big tits." I give Dad a kiss and bolt for the door.

"Gwen," he yells.

"Gotta go. Bye." I whip out the door, grinning over my clean getaway.

⤐

"Gwendoline Isabella."

I don't turn around.

Her running steps get closer as she puffs up beside me. I look at her sideways and, with horror, notice that she's got a tiny, tight ponytail sticking out the middle of her head.

She looks up at mine and says, "I love your hair, dear. Don't you dare change a thing." Clara blinks her long black lashes at me from behind her magnifying-glass lenses.

The elastic holding the ponytail on top of my head seems to tighten. My fingers itch to undo it, but I can't make them move.

"My mother still thinks that she can control my hair," Clara says. "She wanted to try to French braid it. I hardly have any hair to work with and she's always trying to fix it, which is *so* flattering to me. What can I do? I let her do this and I thought it looked gross, but it looks good on you."

I watch my feet as we walk. I've picked up the pace a bit, but she's matching me step for step. "Don't you think, though, that it would be too weird for us to show up together on the second day of school wearing the same hairstyle? I mean, no offense, but it looks like we're trying to be twins. It's not like anybody could become best friends in a day, right?"

She drops her knapsack and starts fiddling with the elastic in her hair.

"Help me out here." She bends down and sticks her head in my direction.

I don't have a choice. I have to undo it. Her

black hair is knotted around the elastic and I'm having an extra hard time because I'm so angry that my fingers are stiff. I can hear Clara sucking in her breath every time I pull too hard.

"Your mom sure knows how to fix it so it stays," I say.

"Did she screw it up? She's got arthritis." She stands up and works at it herself. She sucks in and pulls at the elastic until it breaks. Her short hair falls down but not all the way. One piece is sticking straight up at the back. She smooths down the other bits but misses the piece at the back.

"How's this?" she asks.

"Better," I say truthfully.

"I know it's a mess. I had it cut short in June and then my parents took us to see my great-grandmother in Peterborough. She's ninety and can't tell who we are when we go there. It's so boring. She says to my mother, 'What nice boys you have.' I nearly died. Your hair is good."

I wait for her to say something like Anisha would say after giving me a compliment. Something like, 'You're a good hairstylist. Maybe you can do my hair for me sometime.' But it doesn't come. I wish I had told her about the piece in the back. I try to think of a way to tell her about it as we walk toward school.

I see loner spit-king, J.W. Reane, walking ahead

of us. If only I could be like him, nobody would want to be with me. I could walk by myself and sit by myself and not have to try to think of nice things to say to people I don't care about.

"I sort of know him," Clara says, biting her lip. J.W. sees her and lets loose a wide grin. She walks on ahead while I try not to choke. Figures Clara would know him.

"Gwen," Clara calls. "Aren't you coming?" Now J.W. is waiting for me, too. Clara's piece of hair is waving in the wind. I focus on his dirty yellow hat, her glasses, his spitty arm, her jerky chicken head. I'm paralyzed.

"Hey, Gwen. How's it going?" Marcia steps up beside me. I thank the powers that be for rescuing me from becoming the third member of the freak squad. I smile at Marcia, and for once I mean it. Until she opens her mouth.

"So have you heard anything from Anisha? She's up in Ottawa, right?"

"No, I haven't heard from her." She looks down at my T-shirt and up at my ponytail. A small thrill runs up my spine. I can tell she thinks it's horrible, and her in those huge baggy-assed pants pretending she belongs to some inner city gang. I stand taller and give my head a little shake to make the ponytail bounce. Marcia gives me this sugary, super-fake grin. We pass Clara and J.W.

"Look who's found a friend," says Marcia, jutting her chin in J.W.'s direction as we go by. I keep my mouth shut. "Now that Anisha's gone, it's going to be interesting to see who will become popular this year. Everybody worshiped her. I don't mean that in a bad way. I know you guys were best friends. I mean, she had that Roots suede jacket and she was so funny, pretty and smart and she was so nice to everyone."

She's putting me on. Anisha was not nice to Marcia. We used to laugh so hard at her, and I knew Anisha was being mean because Marcia was flirting with Tony. Tony, Tony, Tony. I was sick of listening to her go on about him.

I should be nice to Marcia to make up for laughing at her so hard. But mostly it's annoying watching her lips flap and her wad of green gum swim around in her mouth.

"Anisha called me in August," she says. "But I wasn't home. We went to Toronto to go to Wonderland and see my mom's friends. Then, when I got home, Anisha was already moved to Ottawa. I wanted to go to the Ex. Wonderland's all families and the guys running the rides won't talk to you…"

Sweat beads on the back of my neck. The trees ring. I shut down and watch Marcia's mouth move. So Anisha called her after we fought. I'm not surprised. Those two should have been friends. They have a lot in common. They're both fake.

I want to beam out of there and into my real life in France, away from people like Marcia.

Clara and J.W. pass us.

"I think Clara will be popular this year," I say.

"Who?"

"Clara." She must have heard me say her name because she turns my way and waves on cue.

"You mean that girl with J.W.?"

"Yes. She's really…" I try to think of a good word. "She's sweet." I wave back at Clara and she gives me her humungous holey smile. Perfect. She still has that piece of hair waving in the wind. I think it's the best hairdo I've ever seen. Marcia's eyebrows are curled around like she thinks I've lost it.

"You think *she's* the next Anisha?" She stands back and hooks her thumbs on her belt loops. I wish I had a handful of something to squish into her sour face.

"Better her than me," I say and walk up the stairs and into the school.

⌁

I have to take down my ponytail after Tim pulls it twice during art. Clara offers to hit him for me, which annoys me more. Why won't everyone leave me alone?

Ms. Lenore tells us that they are going to be adding the new gym to the school this year and that we are supposed to be designing a mural to go on the construction walls. She puts us in teams of four to talk about ideas. Clara takes my arm and bounces up and down in her seat so that Ms. Lenore has no choice but to put her on my team. Then she makes Tony and Tim sit with us. Two girls, two boys. Ms. Lenore is so big on equal everything, as if she could make life fair.

I have to admit that Tony's tan is looking pretty good today. It is going to burn Marcia that he's in my group. If only Anisha could somehow find out about this.

"What happened to your ponytail?" says Tim in this high, teasing voice.

"What do you care?" answers Clara for me.

"Come on, we have to at least fake like we're talking about murals," says Tony. He looks at me, like it's my responsibility to make us work. Then Tim and Clara are staring at me, too.

"Fine, you want an idea? Birds. That's my idea." I sit back with my arms crossed.

"Birds!" says Clara. "Symbols of freedom, birds of a feather, the soaring of the spirit…" She takes off with it. I can tell Tony's eating it up. His chipped front tooth lightly scrapes his lower lip.

"What do birds have to do with a gym? It's

lame." Tim laughs and nudges Tony. Tim has red hair, freckles and his round cheeks are always flushed like he's been running. His shoulders are kind of hunched. He sort of sputters when he laughs and then he has to slurp in.

"Birds of a feather. We can make bird teams," says Clara.

"It's lame. Birds are faggy."

"Why would you say that?" I jump in, sitting forward.

"Feathery, pretty, fluffy, girly, faggy."

"Calm down. It's an idea," says Tony.

"C'mon, Tony. Birds in team uniforms? Might as well have poodles."

"Animals playing sports! That's a great idea. Don't you think, Tony?" says Clara. Tony's got his pen in his mouth, thinking it over. Tim shrugs back in his seat and shakes his head.

"It's not that creative. Disney did it already. It could look infantile," I say. Clara stares at me, then opens her binder and writes the word "Ideas" at the top of the page. Underneath she writes "Birds" and "Animal Teams" and snaps her pen, waiting.

"We have three classes to come up with something. We don't have to go hyper on the first idea," Tim says.

"Then you shouldn't shoot down the first idea, either," says Clara.

"Hey, I'm entitled to my opinion," Tim says.

How long do I have to sit here pretending I care about some stupid mural I'm not going to be around to see? I'll be strolling through the Louvre way before the construction walls are up. What a waste of energy.

"Isn't your dad an artist of some sort?" Tony says. The air around me grows still.

"No, he's an engineer at Dupont," I say. "Who told you he was an artist?" My heart pounds to the beat of some fast song.

"Anisha. She said you had these paintings in your house that your dad did. Portraits of your family. She said they were ultra-realistic, like more real than real. She said I should see them, that I could learn a lot from them. Was she lying?"

He asks me like it's a challenge. Why did Anisha say anything to him? When did she get the chance? What else did she say?

"Is your dad an artist?" Clara asks. Questions. The number one reason I wanted to be a loner.

"We just have some pictures at home," I say quietly.

"I want to see," says Clara.

I think of something.

"How about sports equipment for the mural?"

"Yeah," says Clara. "All different balls." She writes the word "Balls" on her ideas page.

"Balls — you mean like circles with lines on them? That's pathetic," snorts Tim.

"She didn't say balls. She said sports equipment," says Tony. Then Tim starts cracking ball jokes and Clara tells him to shut up. I breathe a sigh of relief that the conversation has moved on. My heart is still racing. I wonder how much Tony knows?

≻

In the four years I hung with Anisha, she came over to my house three times. Her place had a rec room in the basement that we had to ourselves and there was a fridge there, too, so we would make Jello experiments and take them down to go solid while we watched TV, did our homework and worked on dance routines. She always made it so she was in the middle of the pretend stage.

I didn't think she was interested in anything at my house. We ended up there when Dad was on vacation because it was kind of fun to be in the house without adults and the babysitter wouldn't show up until five-thirty. It was strange, though, being in my house with her. I had always wanted her to see my place, but once she was there, I didn't know what to do with her. Being in my house broke the spell of Anisha being in charge. And without her in charge, we didn't know how to be together.

CHAPTER FIVE

DAD AND LEON TOOK ME CAMPING AT Frontenac Park at the end of June. We rented kayaks to paddle to the camp site. A loon passed right by me. A cool wind made the waves choppy and blew us sideways. Trickles of water climbed down my oar and up my sleeve when I tried to back-paddle to correct my steering. Dad dumped in Birch Lake and couldn't get back in his kayak. We tied it to the back of Leon's, and Dad hung on to a rope at the end of the boat and floated on his back with his arms above his head. Leon towed him and the boat the rest of the way to the camp ground, paddling hard. Leon swore at him, but Dad laughed all the way. Most of Dad's stuff got wet and we had to rig up these ropes to hang every-thing around the fire. We sat in close that night, roasted wieners on sticks and breathed in the steam coming off Dad's clothes.

When we got back, I saw the second postcard in

the mailbox and stuck it in my back pocket. I locked myself in the bathroom to read it.

That one was like lightning going through me. I thought for sure…two postcards in two months. This had to be it. I almost told Dad about them, I was so, so sure, but I thought I'd hang on until he got the call. If it was going to happen, if we were going to meet, she would have to call Dad.

It got so that every time the phone rang, I thought, "This is the one, this is the call." But it never was, so I dropped it.

Here's what the second postcard said:

Dearest Gwendoline,

I am still on the move, but hope to settle down soon. I saw an apartment last week that had a bedroom I know you would love. You could almost jump in the river from the window. Unfortunately, it was far, far too expensive. Oh, well. C'est la vie.

I miss you so much.

Love Mom

This one has a picture of a window opening onto a beautiful mountain view. On the back it says that it is a picture of the Swiss Alps, but I think the stamp is French.

It's been almost a week since school started and I haven't gotten any new postcards. I'm probably doing something wrong. I do the spell the same

40

way every time and if I make mistakes I start over. Last night I had to start four times because I couldn't get the box to stand up and the energy went out of the cards. My hands got angry and kept shaking, trying to get the walls up. It only worked after I took a break and breathed deeply for ten minutes before trying again. I started at 11:23 and didn't get to sleep until after one.

Which part of my spell is the working part? It might not be the spell that works. Maybe it was not having any friends this summer that made the post-cards come.

Maybe my mother only communicates with me when nobody else will.

>-

Clara has got into the habit of waiting for me where Raglan meets Patrick so that we can walk to school together. She never asked if it was all right with me. I've tried being early and late, but she's always there.

I can see her singing to herself as I come up the street. She holds her hands in front of her and has this dopey look on her face, like she's in the middle of some sad love song. She stops when she sees me coming.

"Hi, Gwendoline Isabella," she says. She still calls me that.

I grunt. I don't stop for her. I keep moving and

41

she falls in. I'm trying to be a loner and she is ruining it. I promised myself this morning that I wouldn't say anything to her unless asked directly. Clara starts talking.

"My brother took forever to get out of the bathroom this morning. Then I go in there and it reeks. I swear he uses a ladle to put on his aftershave." I clench my teeth. Clara's sniffing her arms to see if she's got any aftershave smell on her. I try to sniff without her seeing me sniffing. I do catch a whiff of a perfumey smell that sticks in my throat.

"My brother thinks he's so hot because this girl called him last night. He was on the phone for over two hours. We were watching TV and we saw two sitcoms and a drama before Dad flipped out. The whole time Garth – that's my brother – didn't say anything. I mean, all he said was 'uh-huh…yeah… sure…get out…get outta here…no way.' Stuff like that." She nods her head like she's the one on the phone talking. She hasn't noticed that I'm not saying anything.

"He didn't use any nouns," she adds. We go about half a block in silence. I'm waiting for her to notice that I'm ignoring her.

"The phone's in the hall by the living room, so we had to listen to the whole stupid thing. Dad said he wanted to watch ER in peace and he flipped out and unplugged the phone. Then Garth stomped

upstairs and slammed his door so hard that a piece
of the hall ceiling came down. It was pretty intense.
I thought they were going to hit each other. During
a commercial, Dad runs up the stairs and knocks
on Garth's door. Garth won't open it, so Dad yells,
'Congratulations on having a girl call you, Garth.'
It was too much."

It's obvious her entire family is crazed.

I can't be her friend. I can't have any friends or
my mother will never call for me. I know it. I know
the postcards have stopped coming because Clara's
trying to be my friend.

We turn the last corner before school. I can see
J.W. Reane up ahead of us, waiting for Clara like
he has something to say to her.

"Uh-oh. I'm not in the mood for him this morning," Clara says, ducking behind me.

"What do you want me to do?" Her breath hits
my right ear. It smells like raisin bread and makes
my stomach churn. I step sideways, but she shifts.

"Cover me, all right? He thinks he can hang out
with me because we knew each other at camp. He's
a nice guy, but he's not my type." We're getting
closer to J.W., who's smiling like it's some big joke
Clara's playing on him. Then I can see it dawn on
him that Clara's maybe hiding. His eyes begin to
turn to the sky. Clara steps on my heel. I take a
deep breath and turn on her.

43

"You're squashing me. Get off." I march past her, then J.W. and run the rest of the way to school.

I see Marcia on the steps talking to Tony. She is standing with her arms crossed in front of her, trying to look casual. I run past them up the stairs.

"Hey, Gwen." I turn at the sound of my name. Tony's looking straight at me.

"Uh. Hey." I run into the building. He probably thinks I know where he can get hold of Anisha. That's what she wants to happen.

Even after we stopped being friends, Anisha made sure that I had her address in Ottawa. I can't believe she remembered where I lived. I answered the door, but I wouldn't let her in the house. I asked her what she wanted and she shoved her new address at me. "In case of emergency," she said, standing on my front stoop. Sure, like the emergency of Tony wanting to talk to her. I closed the door in her face.

Later, I found the paper with her address on it shoved under the doormat.

✂

Ms. Lenore puts us back into our groups to come up with the mural idea. Clara's sitting across from me. I've been avoiding her eyes all day. It's easy in class because I can look straight ahead. But here, we're supposed to talk to each other.

Ms. Lenore wants at least four ideas per

group. She goes on and on and on about what a terrific opportunity this is to show off our young imaginations because the construction walls will be up for a good part of the year. Then she gives us a bunch of her own ideas which mostly include kids of different races stuck in wheelchairs. By the time she's finished blabbing, half the period is gone.

"How does she expect us to do this if she keeps yakking like a beaver," Tim says.

"Beavers don't yak, you idiot," says Clara.

"They've got huge chattering teeth," Tim says.

"Come on, I think this could be cool. Like doing graffiti except it's legal. Everyone's going to see it so we don't want it to end up being some lame-ass thing like flowers with books inside," says Tony.

"That doesn't sound lame-ass," says Clara too loudly. Tony and Tim laugh at her and I have to press my lips together to keep from grinning. "What?" she says. "I thought that sounded like a good idea. But I thought sports equipment was good, too. And birds." I stare at the table and run my thumbnail down a crack in the corner.

"That's what I don't get," I say. "Why do we have to work in groups of four if we're supposed to come up with four ideas anyway? Why couldn't we come up with our own ideas? What do we need

45

the group for?" I'm waiting for them to agree with me, but they look like I told them their goldfishes died.

Tony turns to Clara and they start talking about flowers with books in them. Tim says that if we're going to use books they should be on the backs of construction trucks. They don't seem to notice that I'm not part of the conversation anymore. I sit back in my chair and start drawing a digger being operated by a girl in a wheelchair. Two minutes before the bell is supposed to ring I shove the thing on the table. Clara picks it up.

"Hey, that's good," she says. "You can tell your dad is an artist." I can't believe she's being nice to me after I tore into her this morning. Tony picks the picture out of her hand and nods his head like he has final approval. That thing was supposed to be a joke.

"Yeah, maybe Gwen was right about us each coming up with our own idea. The presentation is next Friday. Maybe we should each come up with something for Tuesday's class." Clara and Tim seem to think that's a good plan. Nobody asks what I think.

After school Clara invites me over to her house to work on our mural ideas together. I stare at the sidewalk.

"I can't," I say. "I'm sorry." She stands there

waiting for me to make an excuse but I can't think of anything that wouldn't be a lie, so I don't say anything. I lift my head a little to try to see what she's thinking.

"Are you mad at me?" she asks.

"No."

"Is something wrong?" she asks. I feel tears beginning to bloom. She's watching me. Clara, with her big eyes.

"Maybe tomorrow then?" she asks.

"Maybe." I walk away. I feel the weight of her eyes on me all the way down Patrick Street, but when I turn to go into my house, she's gone.

CHAPTER SIX

THAT NIGHT, DAD MAKES PIZZA FOR DINNER. He makes the crust himself and rolls it out thin, then stacks it with sausage, red pepper, black olives and extra cheese. He makes it about once a month, sometimes twice if he's in the mood. Usually we eat it on the black beanbag chairs in the TV room and watch a video, but tonight he's got the leftover red Christmas candles going in the dining room like it's somebody's birthday.

"What's going on?" I ask.

"Nothing. Can't a man make his daughter a nice dinner once in a while?" he says.

Something's up. Maybe it happened. Maybe Mom called. Usually I know what's going on in his head. Usually I'm the one telling him what he's thinking. He'll be sitting in the living room reading a computer magazine and clutching his stomach and I'll have to say, "What's for dinner?" to remind him that he might be hungry.

The crust snaps and crunches in our mouths. I wait for him to say what he has to say and he sits there pretending nothing's going on. When he finishes his slice he opens his mouth and I sit up.

"You want another slice?" he says. I can't stand it anymore.

"Dad! When are you going to tell me?"

"What? When am I going to tell you what?"

"About the phone call?"

"Oh, that," he says and wipes his mouth with his napkin. I'm shivering. It happened.

"How could you know about that?" he says. "Fine. I'll tell you. Leon phoned. He's quit his job. He's been thinking about it for a long time, but today's the day he did it. I said he could use the spare room as an office, but only if it's okay with you…"

My mind is going in circles.

"Leon quit?" I say, trying to catch up.

"Uh-huh. His boss was none too happy about it, either. She's bent out of shape because she's afraid he's going to steal some of her accounts."

"And he's going to work here?" In the spare room – he means the ghost room. Now Leon's going to be around *all* the time.

"Yeah, so on the weekend he'll come over and we'll move the bedroom stuff out of there and we'll go get stuff for Leon's office. He's got this mondo

49

computer picked out and we might get a drafting table, too. I think there's room in there for it. So, you don't mind, do you?"

"What?" This whole big pizza deal over nothing.

"We don't absolutely have to do this, Gwen. But, to tell you the truth, I'd be relieved to know he was around when you came home after school. I'm not comfortable with you being here alone. Last year you were always at Anisha's."

"Okay, Dad, I get the point." So that's what this is really about.

"What point?" he says, scratching behind his ear with his long nails.

"I know what you're doing. I know you've noticed that I don't have any friends this year, but you don't have to get Leon to *play* with me. I'm thirteen, Dad. I can take care of myself."

"No, no, no," he says with his mouth full of pizza. "Leon does want to work here. It's okay, right?" He has a big blob of cheese stuck on his chin. You'd think he'd know where his mouth is after forty-one years of eating. I put my finger on my chin to show him he's got something there. He wipes his chin and looks at me like a dog waiting for a bone.

"I said it was okay, didn't I? It's not that big a deal."

"Oh, it's a big deal, all right. You know what a chance Leon's taking, going freelance in this town? He does have a few leads. He'll either start raking it in, or die a long, slow, painful death…as an art director." I shake my head and stare at my plate. I really thought my mother had called him. I thought for sure this time.

"What's wrong, Gwen?" he asks after a while of letting it be quiet. "You were saying you don't have any friends this year. Do you miss Anisha? Is that it?" When it's just me and him, sometimes his eyes go soft. It's like his soft eyes are freshly peeled onions in how they make my eyes leak.

"No. I don't miss her," I say, wiping my nose with my sleeve. "I hate her. She's so ignorant. I can't believe I spent all that time with her." He moves closer and puts his arm around me. He always does that.

"Don't you like the other kids at school? Is anyone…jerking you around? What's going on, sweetie?"

"Nothing," I whisper and shove my head into his chest. He holds on to me for a long time. I look at an olive on the tablecloth and listen to him breathe. Dad kisses the top of my head, gives me a squeeze and lets me go. He wipes my eyes with his thumbs and smiles that goofy lop-sided grin of his.

"I got Heavenly Hash ice cream, too, in case the

51

pizza didn't work. Want some?" He gets up, leaving me to play with the melted candle wax.

The candles are making it hot. I open the dining-room window. The sunset clouds make mountains in the sky above Skeleton Park. That's not the park's official name, but everybody calls it that because it was built on a burial site for victims of a flu epidemic way back when. The neighborhood kids and dogs run and play on the grass growing over their dead bodies. Whenever they have to dig there for the sewers, they always find bones. They put a playground on top of it, but it's still a grave-yard.

Leon can move his stuff into the spare room and call it an office, but that won't change what was there before. Doesn't matter what's in it. That room will always be the ghost room to me.

I open the window wider, lean out and smell the cool air.

➤

Dad and Leon are moving the ghost room furniture out into the truck. Neither of them is really fit, so they are panting like two dogs. I can tell they are trying to prove to each other that they are in good shape by moving everything out fast. I sit on the windowsill and watch them grunt as they lift stuff into the van. The room is naked.

I never came in here anyhow. It had these frills

on everything, little roses on the bedspread and perfume bottles on the vanity. It was too girly a room for me. They took the mirror off the vanity and put it in the TV room. It's going to Leon's place because he doesn't have one. It was an empty mirror. Nobody ever looked in it except by accident. All that mirror ever saw was the room: the empty bureau, the empty bed, the curved top of the empty chair in front of it, and the round, pale-faced wind-up clock that stopped ticking five years ago.

That's when my mother left. The ghost room used to be hers.

Dad said I could have anything I wanted from here. He said I could have the canopy bed. Before she left, I used to love that bed. It was like a fairy-tale bed with the fine white mesh coming down. I did sleep in it once after she'd gone, but I had this horrible nightmare that I started going transparent. In the dream, I was lying on the bed, weakening. My arm felt like it weighed a thousand pounds, only it looked like nothing at all. It was fading, so that I could barely make out its edges. I tried to throw off the covers, but they were too heavy. I looked at my arm and rolled up the sleeve of my pajamas and saw nothing. I didn't exist anymore. It was like I was haunting myself. I sat straight up in the bed screaming.

Ever since then, every time I see those mesh curtains on the canopy bed, I feel like I'm a ghost and my stomach goes empty.

I'm glad they're taking it away.

Leon comes huffing up the stairs and grabs a couple of drawers from the bureau.

"You could help," he says. Sweat pours down the front of his legs below his red bicycle shorts.

"You two are doing fine without me." I look out the window at Dad putting the chair to the vanity in the van. We're taking it to the Goodwill.

"I understand if this is upsetting to you."

"I'm not upset. I'm glad we're getting rid of this stuff. It's not like she was using it. You need a place to work. I understand. It's practical." I squeeze my crossed arms closer to my body.

"It's more than practical, Gwen. I like it here. I want to spend more time with you. That's part of it." A drop of his sweat hits the floor. Dad comes up behind him and I turn to the window again.

"Gwen?" Leon asks.

"What?" I hiss, whipping my head around.

"You okay, Princess?" Dad asks.

"*Don't* ever call me that," I say and walk past them to the bathroom. I lock the door and sit in the dry tub.

"Leave her," I hear Leon say to Dad. I wait for them to go downstairs with the last of the stuff. Then I go back to the ghost room.

54

It's completely empty. You can see the outlines on the walls of where the furniture used to be. When we paint the walls, they'll disappear, too.

୬

We go to the Business Depot to look at office furniture.

"What do you think of chrome, Kevin?" Leon asks Dad.

"Mmm, yes. Chrome. Well, you can see yourself in it," says Dad.

"Good point." They nod their heads like Tweedledee and Tweedledum. I plop myself on an office chair and use my feet to spin it.

Round and round and round she goes. Where she stops, nobody knows. I steady myself long enough to catch them arguing in the corner.

"No, no, no. Absolutely not. Kevin, what are you thinking? You can't be serious. This desk looks like it's wearing a tie."

"It is office furniture, Leon," Dad says. "It should look like it's wearing a tie."

"You're so old-age. Tell your dad to get with it, Gwen," Leon says, trying to drag me into it. I spin away.

And spot Clara coming down the aisle, her eyes widened in excitement like I'm a movie star. She's with her mom who is wearing a straight skirt and one of those blouses with the flouncy ties at the neck, and it's not a work day. Mrs. Scanlan is staring at Leon. I can see her focus on his dyed blond hair. I wish myself to disappear.

Clara comes toward me.

"Hi. What are you doing here?"

"Nothing. Thinking about buying a desk." I try to turn her away from Dad and Leon. Leon is getting loud. I take a deep breath. "What are you doing here?"

"Nothing. Getting videotapes and a binder for Garth. He's grounded because Mom found out he hasn't taken any notes in class since school started. He says he's keeping it in his head, but he's really trying to be cool by not carrying any books. Is that your dad?" Clara is looking over my shoulder at Leon.

"Family friend," I say, tensing.

I bet Dad's looking at us. I'm afraid that Dad or Leon might come over and want to be introduced to Clara. Clara's mom is still giving Leon the evil eye but she's also checking me out like I'm some hooligan.

"I hate getting dragged around all weekend," says Clara. "I mean, it's not like we're kids anymore, right? Why do we have to go all over the place with these guys? It's embarrassing. You see what Mom is wearing? She bought that yesterday and she had to wear it today."

"Clara," Mrs. Scanlan calls. Clara grimaces.

"I might as well be wearing a leash. You do one wrong thing and they're on you like glue." Her mom calls her again. "All right," she calls back. Then she drags her feet down the aisle toward her mother, who is still staring at Leon.

I hear Dad say, loudly, "Leon, over here. What about this one? Look at the legs. Nice, eh? Sexy."

I dig my fingernails deeply into the fake leather armrests and start to spin again.

"Who was that?" Dad asks, stopping the chair.

"This kid from school. They're getting her brother a binder." That seems to be enough for him. Clara's mom turns down the aisle. Clara follows her, turns at the end of the aisle and waves at me. Then she clutches at her neck, pretending she's being pulled by a leash.

"Hammy," says Dad.

I wonder what Clara did to get herself in trouble? Maybe she was talking about her brother.

CHAPTER SEVEN

I LAY THE POSTCARDS ON MY BED EARLY. I used to take the weekend off from weaving the spell. That was before the fight with Anisha. Now I sometimes do it twice on the weekend to make up for the times that I didn't do it before.

I started the spell after the first postcard came. I ran my fingers over the words. The words were clues.

"I think about you all the time. I miss you."

I heard the words run in my head until it was me saying them to her. Then I had the first dream where she touched my face, and I knew that the postcard was her way of touching me. I knew that no matter where she was, I could be with her through the postcard.

I'm not crazy. I understand it's only paper. But it's paper she touched, so I touched it. And the spell came out. It felt like it came from somewhere else — North, South, East, West. It felt like she sent it. Like the postcard it was part puzzle, part clue, part key. She's confused, still. That's why only bits of her are getting through. I knew the postcards were messages asking for my help.

So I spoke the spell, touching the sides of the card, one side for each direction of the compass, so I could reach her wherever she was. There's a reason for every part of it.

When the second card came I knew it was working.

When that postcard mentioned a bedroom, that's how I knew to use the cards to make a room – we couldn't be together in the ghost room that she'd left, so I had to make a new room for us out of the postcards.

The first room was a triangle. I leaned the cards against each other with the writing facing in after I'd charged them with the spell. It was supposed to be like when you face two mirrors together and they can look at each other into forever. I knew the card room was working when the third postcard came.

The third is one of my favorites because Mom talks about me going there for real. It came at the end of July. Also, it was the first that started coming when they started coming one after the other. The third one is like the first drop of rain in a sun shower.

My dear Gwen,

I have a big new apartment and a new job! I'm living with someone so it makes it more affordable. I'm working as a cook at a bookstore downtown. All the bookstores have little coffee shops attached to them. When it's not busy, I can read, but I have to be careful not to get any food stains on the books. I'm saving my pennies so that you can come over. I can't wait to see your shining face again. You are the best girl.

Love Mom

The handwriting is smaller and squished in. This one has a picture of a woman reading. I touch the sides of that one four times. North, East, South, West. Love, love, love, love. Best, best, best, best.

When I'm done, I can hear Dad and Leon talking downstairs, but I can't hear what they are saying. Then I hear them laughing.

I fall asleep and dream I am a crumpled postcard rolling through my house, out of my bedroom, past the bathroom, the stairs to the third floor, the ghost room, the TV room, then bouncing down the stairs and out the door. Then I'm rolling down the street toward school, past hedges and garbage cans, through puddles and over ants. I see Clara coming up on the corner, but she doesn't see me. I hope I can stop long enough to hear what she's singing, but I roll on past. Then I begin to

60

uncrumple in a way that seems fast and slow at the same time, like those clickety old movies. I want to grab at something to stop, but cards don't have hands. Flattened, I see the card is a portrait of myself. It catches against a tree and flaps in the breeze, like a paper flag. The wind tears at my chin, my cheeks, my eyes. Pieces of me churn in a confetti whirlwind. Then, I'm blown away.

⤳

Clara is not at the corner when I get there Monday morning. She could be sick. She could have a doctor's appointment — no, she would have said something. She can't keep her mouth shut about things like that.

It's getting colder out. Soon I'll have to find a warmer ugly loner outfit. I'm running out of grubby old T-shirts.

I pull on my sleeves, try to curl them over my elbows.

Come on, where is she? I'm tired of waiting.

Then it hits me. She's not allowed to walk with me anymore. Her mom took one look at Leon and decided she didn't want her daughter hanging out with a bunch of weirdos.

I didn't want to walk with her anyhow. Stupid blabbermouth geek. Where is she?

I look down the street and stomp my foot.

"Come on," I say out loud.

"Looking for me?" Clara calls from the opposite direction. I immediately start walking while she catches up. "Thanks for waiting," she says. "My dad wanted me to drop off an envelope at the painter's house. She's a painter but she cleans out easedrops, too."

"She cleans out what?" Clara is red in the face and panting from catching up.

"Easedrops."

I can't help smiling.

"You mean eavestroughs, the things where the water runs into them from the roof, right?"

"You know what I mean," she huffs. "You want to come over tonight? We can work on our wall ideas."

"How do you know J.W. Reane?" I'm not sure where the question comes from. I guess I was thinking about how no matter how weird a person is, he or she must have a family and stuff.

"Oh, him," she says. "He was a junior counselor with me at the day camp this summer. The one in Grass Creek Park? I don't think anyone from this school knows about it except for J.W. I used to go to Central, right? That wasn't going to work this year," she says quietly and pauses with her mouth open like she has something to say, but then she seems to change her mind and shakes her head.

"It was St. Matthew's Day Camp and we did

canoes and singalongs, and swam. This girl, Cynthia, had a huge crush on J.W. He was the best at canoes, aside from the counselors."

"Get out!" I gasp.

"It's true. Here it's different. It's like nobody likes him. I could tell, first day. Did he do something?"

I shake my head again. Someone had a big crush on J.W. Reane? I can't wait to tell....For a second I forget that Anisha is gone. She would die.

Clara stops walking beside me, so I stop, too.

"Are you going to come over?" she says.

"Sure. Why not?" Even as I'm saying it, I know it's the wrong thing to say.

⤳

All day long Clara keeps smiling at me like we are sharing some sort of secret. If she says anything about going to her place I'm going to make up some excuse. I'll tell her that I forgot I had to do something for my dad, or that I'm not allowed to go over to people's houses when my dad hasn't met them.

It's nothing against Clara. It's just that I have to be ready for when Mom calls for me to come to France. Maybe once I've been there for a while I can write and explain everything. Maybe she could come to visit next summer if her parents let her. Now's a bad time.

I keep waiting for her to bring it up so that I can tell her, but she never says anything. Then we're walking home and we get to Raglan Street. She turns and I turn with her. I'm getting up the nerve to tell her. She turns again and then I turn and then it's too late to say anything because we're there. I stand outside her door like an idiot, waiting.

"What's the matter?" she says, kicking off her shoes inside. I peer through the screen door.

The house is small, or it seems that way because of all the furniture in it. There's a bunch of dusty coats hanging on hooks inside the door. They didn't put them away for the summer and it's almost fall again. There are dust bunnies in the front hall and a path worn through to the hardwood right down the center. Beside the stairs is the telephone table that Garth must have been sitting at when his father went nuts over wanting to watch television in peace. There are phone numbers written right on the wall beside the phone, and someone has colored in the four corners of the little table with blue ink.

I come in and take off my shoes. The living room is tidy but dusty. I almost ask Clara about it. I mean, her mom seemed so clean but you could knit sweaters from the dust bunnies in the corner of that living room.

I follow her into the kitchen and there's Mrs.

Scanlan drinking coffee, reading a book and wearing the exact same suit she was wearing at the Business Depot on the weekend. Clara rolls her eyes. Her mom is using that same evil-eye look as before, like she's trying to see through my skin.

I notice her book is a murder mystery by an author Dad likes.

"Hi, Mom," says Clara. "This is my friend, Gwen. This is my mom."

I want to leave.

"Was that your dad I saw you with at the store?" she asks. I shake my head, knowing she means Leon. "Who was he, then?" I take a step back. I'm not used to being questioned like this. Clara is waiting for an answer, too.

"He's a friend of the family," I say.

"I've seen him around. He has that look." I take a breath. Mrs. Scanlan is staring at me again. "He looks creative." I breathe out.

"Gwen's dad is an artist," says Clara, and I go on the alert again.

"Oh, really? What's his name?" Mrs. Scanlan asks, taking a sip of her coffee.

Why did I come here?

"Kevin Bainbridge."

"Yes, I think I have heard that name, but I can't think of where. What kind of art work does he do?" My heart pounds in my ears.

65

"Oh, I doubt you've heard of him. He's never had a show or anything. He, you know, fools around at home."

"Fools around at home," she repeats. I don't like the way she looks at me, eyeing me up and down as if I've got something behind my back and she's trying to figure out what it is. I notice she's spilled coffee on the tie of her blouse.

"He does portraits. Of us," I say, desperate to wrap it up. Clara has a couple of ginger ales from the fridge.

"Come on," she says. "Let's go upstairs." I'm grateful to be out from under Mrs. Scanlan's eyes which, I can tell, are following me out of the room.

Clara shows me the house, including Garth's room which is basically a big futon on the floor and a wheelchair with a whole bunch of clothes all over the place.

"He found the wheelchair in the weeds down by the river. Dad figures somebody ripped it off from the hospital and he keeps bugging Garth to take it back, but he's too lazy to do it himself."

Clara's room is a total pigsty, too. Her clothes are piled on this old blue chair with the stuffing coming out. They've been sat on. Her dresser is dusty except for a space in the middle where she keeps her hairbrush, which is growing a head of hair of its own. She's got greeting cards crammed on a bulletin board by her bed and a whole bunch of dolls and stuffed animals stacked in a pyramid against the wall. She grabs a rag doll and flings herself on the bed.

How long do I have to stay here before I can leave?

"So?" says Clara. She's got a doll's arm in each hand and is twirling it through her arms like one of those sideways tops.

"So?" I say, mimicking her. She hits me on the arm with the doll and laughs.

"Gwen, Gwen, Gwen. You are supposed to say something nice when somebody invites you over to her house. You can say anything, anything at all, but it has to be nice." I wonder if this is how Anisha used to feel at my house.

"Well, don't strain yourself," she says and starts pulling at the hair of the doll.

"I, uh, like your bulletin board. Who are those cards from?" Clara's face lights up.

"Some are from the kids in my group at camp. This one's from a guy named Sebastian who was so incredibly cute you would not believe it. He used to go to Central but then his mom got a computer job in California. He wasn't my boyfriend. We just hung out and talked...I bet you've had a hundred boyfriends already."

One of the envelopes has hearts colored in

beside Clara's name. Another one has a lipstick kiss on the inside.

Fish start to swim in my stomach. I open one of the cards and check the handwriting to make sure it isn't Clara's and what I see is the signing line, *"Your best friend, Cyn."* Clara jumps in front of me and snaps the card shut.

"Don't read them. They're private."

"Then what are they doing up on the wall?" I say, sitting on the bed.

"I like to look at them. It is my room."

I find myself counting them and stop after I get to six. Somebody likes Clara. Lots of people do. This is what she wanted me to see. She wanted to rub her good friends in my face. The cards are probably from losers like J.W. Reane, most popular boy at geek camp.

"I don't have any from the girls I used to hang out with at Central. I saw one of them, Julia, downtown when I was shopping with Mom and she pretended not to recognize me because she was with this bunch of skateboarding guys. She walked right past me. I called after her, though. Made her turn around and some others turned around, too, and I could tell they knew what she did. Serves her right. We used to go to the movies, but after that, she can forget it. I've got lots of better friends than her."

68

"Like who?"

"Like you. And like them," she nods toward the bulletin board.

"I get cards, too," I blurt out, trying to make it sound casual.

"Who from?"

I've already said too much. "They're from an admirer." Clara's brown eyes widen to twice their size behind her glasses.

"Ooooooh. Are they mushy?" I can tell she believes me.

"Some of them are a little mushy," I say, biting my lip.

"Does he go on about your eyes looking like limpid pools and stuff?" She leans closer.

"Nah…but there is some stuff about my shining face."

"Wow."

"And stuff about missing me."

"With all his heart," she says, falling back on the bed. "And you don't know who he is?"

"They're from France," I say carefully. I fall back with her. "And they say I'm going to be sent a ticket there someday and that there's a room for me and — "

"Wait, how can you visit someone when you don't know who he is?" Clara sits up.

"I didn't write the postcards. I got them. I'm

only telling you what they say. Don't you believe me?" Our eyes are fixed on each other.

Finally, Clara nods.

"Wow, do you think you would go if he sent the ticket?" she says.

"It would have to be all right with my dad," I say, getting into dangerous territory. "Anyway, they're only postcards. You can say whatever you want on them. Doesn't necessarily mean anything."

Question marks hang in Clara's eyes.

"I mean, it could be someone having a joke on me. Actually, I think they're probably from Anisha," I say, my heart pounding. I never told Anisha about the postcards. I was going to tell her after the other thing, but I never got the chance and now I'm glad.

"Who's that?" Clara asks.

"She's this girl with perfect everything — teeth and hair, and designer everything and good marks. Her aunt took her for a facial and massage once at Piero's and she had this pair of high-cut Docs that they had to order special in her size. She got an A in English on this essay called 'How to Use the Phone.' It was a good essay, funny. The teacher made her read it to the class. She moved to Ottawa. We used to be friends. Best friends...but we got in a big fight and I think she's probably sending me those postcards to try to freak me out. She thinks that no boy could possibly be interested in me. So the postcards are this big tease to get back at me. Any day I'll get one that says SUCKER in capital letters."

Clara's staring at me with furrowed brows.

"What was the fight about?"

"I don't remember what started it. She couldn't take it if things weren't the way she wanted them to be. She was so superficial. She couldn't take a hair being out of place. She was always on about guys and if you tried to talk to her about anything real, she took off. I couldn't talk to her about anything important and I got fed up with her fakeness. So I shut the door in her face. And that's basically it. I'm glad she moved," I say, shrugging.

"Is she the one I hear Marcia talking about? The one Tony liked last year?"

"Yeah, that's her."

"I bet she'd be burnt if she heard that he has a crush on you. As if you need a pretend admirer."

"What are you talking about?"

"You know what I'm talking about, Miss Perfect."

"Don't say that," I say. It's a compliment but it sounds mean, especially after what I told her about Anisha. She's the one like that. Not me. "I'm not

71

like that. Looks don't matter to me."

"Oh, I guess that's how you can stand to be friends with me then."

"Stop it." I pull one of her pillows and smush her with it. "You think you know everything and you hardly know me."

"That's because you hardly ever talk, dear. If you'd talk more then I'd know you. Anyone ever tell you that you're hard to get to know?" she teases, hitting me back.

"Well, don't force yourself," I say, grabbing a stuffed octopus and shaking it on her head. Dust comes out of it and floats in the air. We both giggle.

CHAPTER EIGHT

WE HAVE A CHANCE TO DRAW ANYTHING we want on the side of our school. We could make it the Sistine Chapel of school murals, and what does Clara want to do? She wants to do bugs in the shape of letters spelling out, "Don't bug us while we're building."

I didn't have the heart to try to talk her out of it. She wasn't too impressed by my idea, either, but that's because she doesn't understand it. I want to make the top part of the wall like the top of a circus tent and underneath we'll paint the teachers dressed like clowns juggling and doing tricks. Clara says she doesn't think the teachers will go for it, but I think they'll like it. They're always talking about juggling everything and how the school is like a circus.

I'm explaining it to Dad and Leon at dinner and they are looking at each other in a way that shows that they think it's a stupid idea, too.

"What's wrong with it?" I say, slapping my napkin against the table. We always eat at the dining-room table and use the cloth napkins when Leon's over, like he's a special guest.

"I don't think teachers have as good a sense of humor as you do," says Dad. He got his hair cut today, so it's stubbly. It makes him look ten years younger. I hate it. He looks like a model from the Zellers' flyer. I hope I don't go gray young like him. He likes to say I did it to him, but I remember when he went gray and it had nothing to do with me. I was being so good then to make things go good.

"But it will be so colorful with lots of different areas to look at. I thought about it a lot already and I don't see what's so wrong with it."

"The teachers might think you're saying that they're a bunch of clowns," says Leon, taking a huge bite of potato with some of it squishing out the side of his mouth. Melonhead.

"What's wrong with that? Clowns are funny. People like clowns," I snap. Dad puts up his hand in the whoa position.

"Fine, fine. You do what you think is best," he says.

"Maybe she's right, Kev. I've always found clowns kind of scary with their huge painted-on faces. Teachers can be pretty scary like that.

Especially near the end of the year once the kids have taken another pound of flesh. And people like being scared – "

"Shut up, Leon," I burst at him.

"Gwen," Dad warns, and his warning voice sets me off.

"No! He's the one being rude this time. He's making fun of my idea. He thinks he's the only one who has good ideas. Like, 'I know, I'll work out of that room in Kevin's house. Nobody's using it and it's not like *she's* ever coming back. Dum-de-dum, that's a good idea.'"

"Calm down, Princess – "

"I told you never to call me that." His face is going red. He's scratching behind his ear again. When is he going to cut his nails? His hands look like girl hands.

"You aren't being fair, Gwen. I asked you and you said okay. Leon was trying to…"

"Break the tension," says Leon, which makes me angrier.

"You always take his side," I say. "He's always right and I'm always wrong."

His eyes flash with anger. He's caught up in his own head, chewing on air like he does sometimes when he can't figure what to cough out. I start imitating him, moving my jaw up and down, lip-syncing to silence. Then Leon steps on my foot under the table to get my attention.

I realize what I'm doing and close my mouth.

"I was trying to ease the tension, Gwen," Leon says. "I'm sorry. I didn't mean to upset you. Can we drop it?"

They want a quiet dinner? Fine, I'll be quiet. There's a place on my napkin where the hem has come undone. I run my finger down it, pulling it apart.

After dinner I go upstairs and stop at the door to Leon's office. We painted the ghost walls grassy green at the bottom and sky blue at the top with a brown-like-dirt line running across the wall below the middle. Leon didn't want a carpet so it's bare wood floor. I think it looks stunned.

I go and sit at his drafting table. My legs hang off the high stool. It's still strange to be in here with it changed. I keep listening for the ticking of the old clock.

When I was being good, I vacuumed in here. I crawled under the bed with the vacuum tube and went around the legs. I swept the kitchen floor every day. I washed the bath mats, place mats and cushion covers, polished the brass knocker on the front door and wiped the dust off all the baseboards in the house.

But she left anyway.

I leaf through Leon's big jug filled with markers

and pencils. Maybe the circus idea is a bad idea. Maybe it's as stupid as using bugs to spell words.

"Waiting for me to draw you a clown?" Leon says from behind me. I don't say anything. "Are you still mad at me? You can tell me when you think my ideas are stupid." I turn on him.

"I think your office is stupid." He comes over and holds my ears. That's what he does sometimes. Leon likes to hold my ears.

"What's stupid about it?" he says. I can't think of anything to say so I kick the side of the drafting table. "You can use my stuff if you want," he says. "Remember to put the caps back on the markers. Here. You need some paper?" He pulls out some paper and lays it in front of me.

"You just want me to come up with another idea for the mural," I say.

"You don't have to come up with anything if you don't want. Doodle, or go watch television. I'm saying you can view this office as a problem or an opportunity."

Why do my problems have to be opportunities? Why can't I just hate something? He leaves me alone and goes to watch baseball with Dad.

I stare at the paper. I have to have something for tomorrow that will beat whatever Tony is going to come up with. He thinks he's so smart and everyone else buys into it. I'm way smarter than he is.

I'm the only one who knows the truth about what's going on. Clara's wrong about him having a crush on me. I know he thinks I'm reporting things back to Anisha. And I know everyone thinks I'm going to go for him now that she's gone. Just because Anisha liked him doesn't mean I have to. Nobody knows we aren't friends anymore and he's still talking about her. She's the pretty one. She's the funny one. She's the one who's super perfect.

Wait. That's it. I run to my room to get the card.

✕

I wake up at 5:16 thinking about my mural idea. I sit up with a start. I forgot to do the spell. Through my big front window I can see a brightening gray between the branches of the trees that line the street. I race to my drawer to get out the postcards. If I do it before the sun comes up, it'll be like it is still night. It'll be okay.

North, South, East, West...

It's getting lighter and lighter.

I try to go fast, but I keep messing it up and have to start again. I always get hung up on post-card number four.

It came in the first week of August. The front is an abstract painting with a blue background and a red swirl in it. The two colors seem to vibrate off each other, they're so bright.

Hi Gwen!

I'm on vacation in Spain with my roommate. The hot chocolate here is like pudding, I thought of you when I ate it. We're staying at a big hotel where they leave wine in your room whether you ask them to or not. They call french fries patatas fritas here. Oh well, time for siesta. When you come we'll come here, okay?

Your Loving Mom

When I come? It's never going to happen. On vacation in a big hotel in Spain? She was supposed to be saving pennies for me to go there. The roommate must have paid. Maybe the roommate is rich. But then why wouldn't he pay for me to go over? Maybe they won the vacation. I'm supposed to go there — that's what it still said. How could I have forgotten to do the spell last night? I'm so stupid. It's the one thing I absolutely have to do, and I forget to do it.

I'm crying and getting the postcards wet. It's almost six by the time I get the box built. The sun is almost up. I've finished, but I don't know if it will work. Something good has to happen soon for me to know it's working.

I'm putting back the postcards when I hear someone. I stop in the middle of the room and listen, trying to hold my breath. I hear footsteps make their way down the hall and into the ghost

79

room. I dive for the bed and pull the covers over my head. My cheeks are still hot with tears. I hear the ghost room's floorboards creak.

That room is cursed. I should tell Leon. Anyone who spends time in that room is in danger of disappearing a little bit at a time. First you forget, then you go transparent, then you aren't there anymore.

I turn over and try to go to sleep. If I sleep and wake up, it'll be like I did do the spell last night after all. If I sleep and wake up, it'll work.

CHAPTER NINE

Ms. Lenore has broken us into our groups again and now she's gone to the "office." That means she's calling her boyfriend.

Tim is bugging Clara about J.W. Reane because he saw him talking to her in the hall.

"I'm amazed you managed to have a conversation with that guy and not get wet," he says.

"What?" Clara says.

"Didn't Gwen tell you? Around here J.W.'s known as King Spit," Tim says. Tony pokes him in the arm to get him to stop.

"Sounds to me like Tim's jealous," I say to Tony.

"She's right, Tony. She's got me." Tim turns to Clara and takes her hand in his. She looks like she's shaking hands with a cockroach. "I have a confession to make, Clara. I have a secret love…and it makes me crazy when I see him talking to anybody else." Clara starts pulling her hand away, but Tim won't let her go. "That's right. I'm

81

in love with J.W. and I'm going to have to ask you to stay away from him. My heart can't take it. You don't want to break my heart, do you, Clara?" She snaps her hand out of his grasp and he falls to one knee in front of her chair. "Please. I beg you. Don't break my heart."

Tim grabs on to Clara's leg and she starts shaking it to get him off, yelling, "Get off, weirdo." By this time the whole class is laughing.

Marcia comes to the classroom door and peeks in. When she sees that the teacher's gone she comes straight up to our group. "What's so funny?" she says, smiling like she's part of the joke. That's when we shut up. She's wearing another one of those shirts that shows off her innie belly button.

"I was going to the washroom and I heard you guys laughing…Math is sooo boring. I can't figure it out. Do we need algebra for shopping? I don't think so. Like the problems are so strained. Nobody can figure it out except J.W."

Tim guffaws. Marcia's tangerine hair is done the same way that Anisha used to do hers, with the two barrettes at the front and then in pigtails. She's looking at Tony who's looking at Tim who's looking at Clara.

I was right about Tim being jealous. Look at him looking at Clara! He likes her.

I remember what I said to Marcia about Clara becoming the most popular girl in the school. I thought I was joking. How can Tim like Clara? I mean, she's nice but she's got those glasses and her shorts ride up between her thighs when she walks. Her jagged black hair looks all right against her smooth skin, I guess. She's not ugly, but she's not Marcia.

"Hey, Marcia, when are you going to put that thing away?" I point to her belly button. I wait for the laugh, but everyone just sits there.

Then Ms. Lenore comes back and everyone goes quiet. Marcia backs out of the room, her arms crossed over her bare midriff. Ms. Lenore starts touring the groups and everyone starts talking again – except my group. I'm staring at the table, but I can feel them looking at me.

"So did anyone come up with an idea for the mural?" Clara says.

Tony opens his binder, and there are these beautiful sketches.

"Wow," I say before I have a chance to think.

Tony's idea is that we do Canadian wildlife, with each part of the construction wall representing a different Canadian region. So for the Maritimes he has lobsters, for central Canada he has beavers, moose and wolves. He has polar bears for northern Canada, buffalo for the prairies, and the west coast gets grizzlies and gray whales. He has drawn the animals in pencil crayon so you can almost hear them breathe. You can see the muscles in the wolf's legs, and the moose, standing in a clearing of trees, looks like it is about to walk straight into the classroom. He pressed hard on the pencil crayon so the colors are bright.

Tony sits back while Tim and Clara go over his mini-masterpieces. Clara keeps flipping back to the beaver.

"He's so cute," she says.

"Thanks. You guys gave me the idea last week. Animals don't need to wear uniforms to get strong. They're naturally strong. Does your dad draw animals?" he asks me.

"No...you must have worked all weekend on those," I say, thinking about how I wasted that hard work in the ghost room.

"I did them in front of the TV." He shrugs.

"Liar," says Clara. "You worked hard on these."

"Yeah, don't lie, Tony," says Tim, mocking Clara. Then he pulls out his drawing of spaceships with books in them. It's in pen and ink on lined paper, and the stars are the kind you can draw in two seconds without lifting the pen from the page. The spaceships are straight lines with semi-circles on top and little swirls of smoke coming out the back.

84

Tim is beaming with pride. "*That* was done in front of the TV," he says. We giggle. "Besides, I thought the idea was that we come up with an idea. I didn't know browner boy here was going to go whacko with the pencil crayons. Maybe mine's not Michelangelo like Tony's, but it's still a good idea."

"Yeah. That's what I thought, too," says Clara, pulling out her Don't Bug Us While We're Building idea.

"That's a good idea," says Tim, taking the picture from Clara and holding it close to his nose to see if he can smell the marker on it. At least she used markers and colored in the whole page. Tim puts the page down and they turn to me.

"Okay, okay." I unfold my piece of paper.

"Hey, that's not what you said you were going to do," says Clara.

"I know, but – "

"Look at this," says Ms. Lenore, pulling the page out of my hand. "Class, everyone quiet down for a moment. Look at what Gwen has done here. This is some original thinking at work. See? Gwen has a number of children here dressed up as superheros. It's simply sketched out on the page, but that's all right. This is exactly what I want. This is what we call a concept. That's great, Gwen." Ms. Lenore puts her hand on my shoulder. I can feel the squeeze in the edges of her long nails. Then the bell rings.

>-

Lunch works like this. I go to sit alone in the lunch room and then Clara comes and sits with me. I didn't used to count it as sitting with someone because I didn't choose to sit with her, but now that I've been to her house, it's stupid to pretend we aren't friends.

How can I tell if my spell is working? Maybe what's happening is what is supposed to happen. It could be I'm supposed to become friends with Clara. It could be that's what the spell made happen. She came out of nowhere. That's magic, right? Maybe she's been sent here to keep me company while I wait for Mom to get the plane fare together.

Everything will be great when I get to France. Mom will do my hair like Mrs. Scanlan does Clara's. I'll compliment Mom's clothes and she'll tell me I'm pretty. I'll go to visit her at the book store and help her in the back cutting tomatoes and onions. I'll wear a white apron and she'll call me Angel.

"Earth to Gwen."

"Huh?"

"Hello? You were a billion miles away."

"No. A few thousand actually," I say, mostly to my sandwich.

"That's giganormous," Clara says, staring at my salami and mozz on crusty bun that Dad made me this morning. He makes me these sandwiches as big as my head.

The lunch room is so loud. It smells like burnt rice in here today. Sometimes I pretend that we are inmates in Kingston Penitentiary. The walls are gray with a puke-yellow stripe near the top. The windows have that wire mesh over the outside to protect them from balls hitting them. They haven't been washed the whole time I've been at McBurney. The boys sit with the boys and the girls sit with the girls and J.W. Reane sits by himself at the small table in the corner behind the pillar.

All lunch long Clara talks about what she eats and doesn't eat. I swear, she has two subjects: her brother and food.

"I wasn't going to have lunch today, but then I read where it can be bad if you don't eat. Your body thinks it's starving and starts saving any little crumb of food you put into it. Wouldn't it be cool if your body was a big fridge that held everything you'd ever eaten? Like there was this amazing carrot cake my dad made a couple of years back. I sure could go for that again. If my body was a fridge I could open up my stomach and get it."

"That is so disgusting," I say. "It wouldn't come out like a triangle piece of cake." Clara looks down at the yogurt she's brought for lunch. She stabs it with her spoon.

"I can dream, can't I? I'm not perfect like you, Miss Big Sandwich Eater." I wish she'd stop that.

Tony and Tim pass by with their sandwiches. I see Clara checking out their food.

"So, did your dad help you with that idea?" asks Tony, barely curbing the edge in his voice.

"I have a mind of my own," I say. It's almost a lie, though. I got the idea from the card Leon made for me.

"It's not a competition," Clara says.

"Yes, it is," says Tim.

"Yeah, but we're in the same group," I point out.

Tony pulls on Tim's sleeve and they move off to the table where the boys sit and try to impress each other with how much they know about sports and computer games.

I look across the room at J.W. Reane sitting alone reading a book and eating fettuccine out of an old cottage cheese container. He's bent over it, shoveling the pasta into his mouth. He doesn't finish one bite before he shoves another one in.

I look at Tony's table again and spy Marcia on her way over to them from her table of Marcia worshipers. Marcia's looking at Tony like he's the special of the day.

"Will she ever give it up?" Clara says. "I mean,

88

can't she tell he's got a crush on you?"

"He does not, Clara. You saw how he was in art this morning right after Marcia left. I make a joke about her belly button and he and Tim act like I punched her."

"It was the way you said it."

"How was that?" I ask. Clara shrugs and then shakes her head. I can tell she wants to say I sounded mean, but she's too nice. "The point is, Tony was on Marcia's side. That proves he doesn't have a crush on me."

"My dear girl. You don't think he spent all that time on those pictures to impress Ms. Lenore, do you? It's so obvious. Hey, when are you going to invite me over to your house? I want to see your dad's art."

I can't think past what she said about Tony.

He can't like me. My dear girl...Nobody talks like that. Clara's crazy. I stare at Tony's table.

Tony listens to Marcia and nods into the table.

"So?" says Clara.

"So what?"

"Can I come over some time?"

"No," I say real fast. Clara's face collapses. Her glasses travel down her nose so that I can't see her eyes. "Sorry. I can't have people over. It's like a rule." It's my rule. "I could come to your house again."

"Not tonight."

"Why not?"

"We're going out to visit this person. A friend of a friend. Have to put on a good show so she can see how happy we are. You know how moms are," she says, trying to penetrate my brain with her stare. I haven't been able to tell her about Mom yet. I can't.

"Ask if you can stay over on Friday," she says, pushing her glasses back up onto her face. "We can camp out in the living room. Dad has this tent that doesn't need spikes. It poofs up on its own. *Poooooooof.*" Clara makes a sound like blowing up a balloon and puffs out her arms as wide as anything.

"Ting." I prick the air in front of me with a pretend pin. Clara, on cue, pops and shrivels down to size, picks up her spoon and eats her yogurt.

"I hate this stuff," she says.

"Here." I pass her half my sandwich and she bangs her hand against her chest as if to say, For me?

"Take it, you big hammy weirdo," I say, as she tears at the sandwich like a starving hyena. "I couldn't stand watching you watching me eat it anymore."

CHAPTER TEN

I CHECK THE MAILBOX WHEN I GET HOME,
but all we have is a circular. I flip through the pages
of coupons. Carpet cleaning, furniture polish, an
oil change, a free haircut and a bucket of chicken,
but no postcard from my mother.

Rule 1. Don't tell anyone about the postcards. If
anyone knows it will break the spell. Rule 2. Touch
every side of every postcard in order every night.

I told Clara that the postcards were from an
admirer, so even though I was talking about my
postcards, she still doesn't truly *know* about them.
And I did do the spell before the sun came up.
Technically, I haven't broken the rules.

Leon's laughing his head off on the phone with
someone. I go to the ghost room door. His back is
toward me. He has his music on low – something
with trumpets. I can hear it echoing lightly off the
floorboards. He's looking out the window and
combing his fingers through his hair like he does.

His papers are all over the place and his printer is chugging away trying to print out some huge copy of a logo he's working on.

I go to my room and pull out the postcards. The fourth one came a week after the third one and the fifth one came a week after that. The fifth one made me feel like it might be okay to tell Anisha about them, because I'd be gone soon enough and then it wouldn't matter what anyone thought.

It's a picture of the harbor at Marseille. I've never seen so many boats in the same place, a forest of sailboat masts reaching for the craggy edges of the cliffs that surround them. The writing is smudged.

Gwen Darling,

Here we are exploring the Mediterranean Coast. My roommate has brought me with him on a business trip. He is sitting across from me having a glass of wine as we watch the sun go down. Sometimes children have wine with dinner here. I'm sure it would be okay with your father if I let you have a taste when you come to visit. My roommate says that you are welcome any time. I will have to talk to my boss about vacation time. Soon, angel, soon.

Love Mom

Soon, it said. It's been almost a month and there's been nothing.

I was going to lean out a window in Paris and

92

breathe in the smell of the river. I was going to drink wine with dinner on a sailboat in the Mediterranean with Mom and the roommate. They were going to buy me French books from Mom's store to take with me when we went to Spain. I was going to make my spoon stand up in a cup of hot chocolate in Barcelona.

Soon, angel, soon.

"Knock, knock," Leon says. He's standing in the doorway of my room. I throw a pillow over the postcards.

"What do you want?" I ask.

"Just saying hi," he says, walking in. I put my leg over the pillow.

"Hi," I say, mocking his voice.

"How was school today?" he asks, sitting on the bed. I put my hand on my knee over the pillow.

I take a deep breath before answering. Leon's hand is right next to my leg. "Uninteresting. Okay?" He clucks his tongue.

"Where'd you pick up that attitude?" He catches my eye and we have a stare-down contest. Usually I can't help but start laughing because who can stand it when Leon tries to get serious. Not today, though. I look up at the ceiling like J.W.

"I can see where I'm not wanted," Leon says and gets up.

"Took you long enough," I yell at the closing door.

I pick up the pillow and cover my head with it. I could suffocate. That would show them. That would show them all.

⤞

Clara stands at the corner, leaning against the hydro pole, singing her heart out. She sees me coming and her mouth shuts into a smile. I get to the corner and, without me saying hi, she falls in step beside me.

"I brought a sandwich today. Mom was having a hissy fit because she said that I made her buy those yogurts for nothing. But I said, 'How was I supposed to know it was going to taste like wet snot,' and then she wouldn't talk to me. Garth thought it was pretty funny. He was nice to me all night. You don't have any brothers or sisters, right?"

I shake my head.

"You're awfully quiet today, dear," she says. "Your mom chew you out?"

"No," I say. I stumble over a crack in the sidewalk. Step on a crack and you break your mother's back. That's how the rhyme goes. Crack, crack, crack. I widen my step.

"You never say anything about your mom." She says it like it's a question. I step on a crack on purpose. And then another. I jump on a third one with both feet.

"I don't have a mother, Clara." I take a deep breath to shove the knot of tears back down my throat. I keep my head down and keep moving. It's been this way for five years. You'd think I'd be able to handle the question.

"What do you mean?" she says, stopping. We're three blocks from school. I want to keep going. I want to walk right past this conversation, but Clara's not going to move until I say something.

"I mean that I don't have a mother at home."

"But what happened? Did she die? Where is she?" I leave her there and start walking again. "You have to have a mother, Gwen. Unless you're an alien," she calls after me. It's such a Clara comment that I have to stop. "You'd tell me if you were an alien, wouldn't you?" She catches up to me and loops her arm through mine.

Half of me wants to shake it off and half of me wants to squeeze it in. I look at the gap between her teeth and stick my pinky finger in it. I've wanted to do that since we met. She spits it out.

"Ewwww, you are a cosmic weirdo, dear."

I take a deep breath.

"My mom's gone. She left when I was eight." I stand there with my heart pounding like a sledge-hammer as Clara's face melts.

I wish I could press Rewind and start this day again.

I try to suck the tears back. Clara's still got my arm.

"We don't have to go to school," she says softly. I turn my head away from her and spy Marcia Whittaker's red-and-blue striped pullover up the street.

The last person I told about my mother leaving was Anisha. We were at her house sitting in her bedroom that had matching pillow cases, sheets and duvet and twelve of those expensive fashion dolls that come with their own stands. I tell Anisha about how my mom took off when I was eight and she plumps one of her pillows and says, "She should at least send you some money." Like that would make it okay.

I feel the heat of my cheeks with the back of my hand.

"We could go to the park and talk if you want," Clara says, patiently squeezing my elbow.

"I'm not that big a mess, Clara. It's not like she left yesterday or anything." I can't stand the look on her face, like I'm a pound puppy or something. "Besides, we have to figure out the mural presentation today and I want Tony to suffer because of my idea being better than his."

"It's supposed to be the team's idea, Gwen."

"Yeah, whatever." I lurch forward and her hand is yanked off my arm. I sigh, step back, pick up her hand and squeeze it back into the loop of my arm.

Do I have to do everything?

><

We're supposed to be working on math problems, but I can't stop thinking about my mural idea. Tony's pictures were good, but the assignment wasn't about the pictures, it was about the idea. My idea is the best idea. And everyone in the school will be painting the mural, so it doesn't matter how good one artist is.

I want to do the superhero thing. At least, I want to do my own superhero.

I sketch an eye on the back of my page of problems. If I could have one superpower it would be the power to make people see. I draw a house in the eye. My house. I don't know how the power would work. Maybe I could put my hands over people's eyes and light would come out of my hands and they could see the light. I draw another eye and inside it I put the Eiffel Tower. Some people would be scared of me, because some people don't want to see. But good people, seekers, would flock to me, asking me to put my hands on their eyes so that they could see the light. I draw an army of stick people marching between the two eyes.

How would I show that superpower? Give the

superhero yellow hands? Clara looks sideways at my page and I flip back over to the math problems.

We get to art class and I'm primed to shove my idea down Tim and Tony's throats so that they'll agree to present it. But before I can say anything, Tony holds his binder above his head.

"I think we should do superheroes," he says. Clara looks at me with her mouth open and I-told-you-so eyes. I kick her under the table. "I was thinking about it last night and I had to admit it was the best idea."

"Did it hurt?" I say with a sneer. Clara kicks me under the table. Tony grins and opens his binder to show how he's made sketches of us as superheroes. As if my picture wasn't good enough.

Then he flips to the one he did of me.

"What do you think?" he says.

I like him. Deeply. For one second.

He's drawn me with my hair flowing and he's given me this heavy-duty tool belt with different-colored paints and crayons stuck in where the tools would go. He's put me in a pantsuit with swirls of color. It's sort of like the one Leon did of me only my boobs aren't so big and Tony got my eyebrows right so they don't seem so surprised.

"Amazing," I say and then catch my cool. "Who am I supposed to be?"

"Creative Woman."

"I'm not that creative." I can't stop looking at the picture. Is this how he thinks of me?

"It was your idea," Clara says, grabbing the binder from me.

The next picture is of Clara. Tony has her wearing x-ray glasses that shoot out rays. Clara's superhero hands are in fists and she's punching the air with one of them as she flies toward a school bus. She's wearing a kilt.

"Not a practical outfit for the flying superhero," Clara says. She sounds disappointed. Tim moves his head into the page, as if he's trying to look up her superhero skirt.

Tony grins wider and flips the page again. He drew Tim like the Joker with a huge evil grin, green skin and red hair.

"I look like the Grinch with a sunburn," says Tim.

"That's exactly what I was going for," says Tony.

"Where's yours?" Clara asks.

I can hardly wait. Bet he drew himself with bulging muscles and a cape.

"I don't know what my superpowers are going to be yet," he says. I don't say anything, but what's going through my head is that Tony *is* a superpower.

CHAPTER ELEVEN

"ARE MY GLASSES ALL THAT ANYONE notices about me?" Clara asks on the way home.

"I thought the pictures were good. I can't believe Tony made them up so fast."

"I'm getting contacts next year when my mom gets promoted and we get benefits. I'm not always going to have these stupid things," she says.

"Come on, Clara. It's for the presentation. It's not like you have to be X-ray Woman for the rest of your life."

"I bet you wouldn't mind being Creative Woman for the rest of yours. Bet Tony draws himself as Creative Man." She makes smooching noises at me.

"Stop it," I say, pushing at her. She steps back a little too fast and turns down Raglan without waving.

"Hey," I yell after her. "I'm going to ask tonight about staying over at your place tomorrow, okay?" She nods.

I start jogging. I can't wait to tell Dad and Leon that the group picked my idea.

The leaves crunch like cornflakes under my feet. I love fall. I love the way the air smells like it's been scrubbed and rinsed with cold water.

When I get home Leon is sitting at the kitchen table staring into his cup of tea with his hand on his chin. I sneak up behind him and put my hands over his ears.

"Hi, Gwen," he says. I clap my hands back and forth over his ears. He sits up and starts humming to the rhythm of my hands on his ears. "Howwww wassss schoool tooodaaayyayay?" I sit down and grab his tea. The cup slides from his hand without a fight.

"Clara says Tony has a crush on me, but I'm not the least bit interested in him. Marcia wants him. You should see – she's all over him. She can have him. He acts like he's the automatic leader of everyone because he's tall. I showed him up today in art class, though. Thanks to you and that card."

"What card?" says Leon. He seems half here.

"Melon. Melony. You gave me the best idea for the mural. I did superheroes. Here." I pull the concept picture I did out of my bag and pass it to him. "We don't need it anymore because we're using Tony's pictures. He drew me as Creative Woman, for some reason. It was a pretty good picture. But the idea was still mine. I mean, I borrowed it from you but it was my idea for the mural." Leon's eyes go dewy and droopy. He leans over and kisses me on the head.

"Thanks, Gwen. This is great. Can I have it?"

"Yeah...are you all right?" He gets up and walks over to the counter. He picks up something and my throat goes dry. He turns around and hands me a postcard.

"This came for you today. I tried not to read it, but I couldn't help myself." He's still got his arm dangling in the air with the postcard at the end of it.

"Did you tell Dad?" I manage to spit out. Leon shakes his head.

I snatch the thing out of his hand and run upstairs to the bathroom. Breathing hard, I lock the door, sit down in the bathtub and close the curtain.

It's a picture of Beauty and the Beast from EuroDisney. Which one am I supposed to be? I want to turn it over, but I don't want to turn it over. I can't believe Leon read it. I slam my fist against the side of the tub. It makes a small, cold thud.

I turn the postcard over.

Dear Gwen,

I looked up at the calendar and realized we are halfway through September already and you must be back in school.

This summer's been so lovely, I thought it would last forever. But, of course, you have school and that's the most important thing. You're so smart, I bet grade 7 will be a breeze. Anyway, you don't need a visit here mucking it up. Maybe Christmas, huh? My roommate will be out of town then so we could have the place to ourselves. Wouldn't that be nice?

Love Mom

I get up and listen at the bathroom door. I open the door, go to my room and hide under the covers.

I thought I was staying inside the rules of the spell, but I must have broken it. I broke it when I told Clara I had a secret admirer. I broke it by forgetting to do it that night. I broke it by letting Leon move in. I broke it by having friends.

Maybe wanting other things was enough to break the connection. I should have wanted her and nothing else.

I plunge my head under the pillows and wipe my nose on the sheet underneath. She must have felt me breaking the connection. Why would she want a greedy teenager to come live with her and ruin things with her new boyfriend?

How can she think I'm starting grade seven? She doesn't even know how old I am.

I sit up, grab the postcard and fling it at the door. It hits Leon in the head.

"Get out," I yell.

"No, I want to talk to you." He picks up the card. I pull the duvet over my head. He sits and tugs at the duvet.

"That isn't the first thing you've got from her, is it?" I don't answer. "I know it's not. You can tell."

"You shouldn't have read it. It's none of your business." I pull at the duvet cover until it threatens to tear.

"Are you going to tell your dad?" he asks, putting one hand on the edge of the duvet so that I can't pull at it so hard. I shake my head.

"Don't you tell him, either. Promise?" He doesn't answer. "I don't want him to know. Please, Leon? If he knows, he'll want to do something and...I don't want them to stop coming. This is the sixth one, okay? And she's never called or anything. She's not going to do anything. They don't make any difference anyhow. Only to me."

"Six? She's sent six letters to you without your dad finding out?"

"Not letters. Postcards. I don't even have her address," I hiss. I can see the steam rising in his face. He never liked her. "Please, Leon, promise you won't tell him."

"Why not?" He stands up and starts pacing the room. "Why shouldn't he know? You're his daughter. We're the ones who take care of you. We're the

104

ones who are here every day. We're the ones who take you camping and buy you clothes and make sure you brush your teeth…and love you. Don't you think we have a right to know about this?" His voice is getting angrier by the minute.

"They're mine. She sent them to me!"

"Yeah," he says. "You're right. A postcard from Disney World is worth so much more than five years of giving a shit every single day, Gwen."

Then we both hear the downstairs door open. It must be Dad.

"Promise me," I say quickly. He stands there huffing with his hands on his hips. "Come on, Leon. She's never going to do anything anyway." I hear footsteps on the stairs. I beg Leon with my eyes. The footsteps are coming straight down the hallway toward my room.

Leon scoots over to the bed. Dad pops his head in. He's smiling. He likes it when me and Melon pretend to get along.

"What's going on here?" he asks. I give Leon a kick.

"Nothing," he says in a way that implies that something is definitely going on. "Girl talk. Someone has a crush on Gwen." I kick him again.

"Who?"

"No one, Dad."

"Oh, right. Sorry. I forgot," Leon says, giving

105

me a wink. "No one has a crush on Gwen. Right? Especially not Tony."

"LEON!"

"Oops. Did I let something spill? So sorry. I'm not like you. I can't keep a secret for long." Dad beams cluelessly on, like a dog ready to play.

"I was thinking of ordering from that Cambodian place. Who's in?" he says. I stand up on the bed, bounce off and make for the door.

"Here, I'll look up the number for you." I make my way past him and run down the stairs to the kitchen. My hands are still shaking as I flip through the Yellow Pages.

⊁

We got through dinner without Leon saying anything. He did watch me like a hawk the whole time, though, as if he had Clara's x-ray eyes and was shooting beams at me to make me tell. Dad thought he was trying to get me to talk about Tony.

"Leon wants to know what this Tony looks like," Dad said.

"He looks like none of your business."

"We know one thing," Dad said.

"What?"

"He's got good taste."

I dropped my fork on my plate and reached for the hot sauce.

"Stop acting touched by an angel, Dad."

"Yeah, Kevin. Don't act so touched," Leon pitched in. I was about to tell him to shut up when he turned his rays on me again. That's when I knew he wouldn't tell.

He's saving it. I'm on the hook.

Now I'm sitting on my bed, turning over the postcards and wondering about my mother. She's a ghost in my life. It wasn't just the dream in the ghost room that made her a ghost. It's this way she has of haunting me with the postcards and through the portraits of us all over the house. The ones I told Anisha Dad painted. I couldn't tell her the truth about them.

I can hardly look at them, because *she's* in them. She's gone but her eyes are everywhere. Dad thinks he's doing me a favor keeping them up. She took all the photographs. I used to think that was because she wanted to remember me. Then, after a while I began to think she took them because she wanted me to forget her. I hardly remember the real her anymore.

I remember a long, soft face with a sharp nose, frizzy blonde hair pulled back into a ponytail, fine fingers on white hands, pointy knees and the smell of those menthol cigarettes she was always trying to give up.

I remember holding onto her purse while we

walked along Princess Street. Icicles made small frozen mountains on the sidewalk with holes in the top big enough for my pinky finger. No time to stop. She walked so quickly, whole neighborhoods whizzed by as I skipped to try to keep up with her. I used to put on her tall boots and see how fast I could run up and down the stairs. Down to the hall and then back up to her room.

The ghost room. I remember the dried petals from old roses on the bureau beside the clock that had to be wound. "Where's the key for the clock?" she said. I had lost it behind the radiator. She was angry that time. Her crying in the kitchen. "Don't look at me," she said. The locked bathroom door with the phone cord leading into it.

Every year I lose a little more and have to make stuff up. I'm not sure anymore what's real about these memories and what's not.

That's why I can't tell Dad. If I told him about the postcards he would want to do something. He'd want to find her and if he did — if he found her and made the ghost of her come real — she might run again. And then all I'd have are the portraits Leon did of us.

The portraits. That's how Dad met Leon. It's funny that it was Mom's idea to hire him.

I mean, she couldn't have known what was

108

going to happen when she picked Leon to do the paintings.

I pull at the corners of the postcards until fibers of paper fray onto my fingers. My mother. My mother my. Mother. Moth hair. "North, East, South, West. Who is the one who you love the best. Not me. Not me."

I lie back with the postcards on my chest right under my nose. I breathe in the smell of them, flat and empty. Moth hair.

I close my eyes and try to picture hers, but dream of Clara's instead. I dream Clara sees right through a ghost me with her x-ray eyes. Then, using her superpowers, she turns me from transparent to real. In the dream, it takes five years for her powers to work and I wait, with my yellow hands over my closed eyes.

CHAPTER TWELVE

"YOU WERE IN MY DREAM LAST NIGHT," I tell Clara when I get to the corner the next morning. She's wearing a wrinkled blue shirt with the buttons done up in the wrong holes. I point at her shirt, and she drops her knapsack and rebuttons her shirt with tight, jerky fingers.

"Yeah, so, what was I doing? Stuffing my face with eclairs or shooting x-rays at people through my big-ass glasses?" Her voice makes me cringe. I don't think I ever thought of Clara as having any problems. I've thought of her more as being a problem.

"Are you still mad because of Tony's picture?" I ask softly.

"No. Yes. I don't know. Why does everyone think of me like that?"

"Like what?"

"Don't pretend you don't know what I'm talking about." She glares at me. "You weren't exactly

110

crazy about being friends with the lumpy new girl."

"But I am friends with you." We walk half a block up the hill toward Skeleton Park. She is stiff beside me. "Come on, Clara. Maybe I didn't want to be your friend at first, but that's because I decided I was going to be a loner this year, because of what happened with Anisha. So if I seemed unfriendly, that's why. Besides, you didn't give me much of a choice about it." She's still not answering. "Why did you want to be friends with me?" It's what I've been dying to ask ever since she changed seats to be beside me in art.

She slouches against a tree, like she's exhausted from climbing the hill. The wind is up this morning and it flips her short dark hair off her face. I can smell the lake on the air. My elbows are cold. I cup them with my hands.

"It's like this, dear," she says. "I'm the new girl, right? I wanted new friends. I wanted a chance to change everything. I saw Marcia and pegged her right away as Miss Superficiality, which I was one hundred percent right about. Then there you were, hiding behind a tree, laughing at Marcia and I thought, 'She knows.'"

"Knows what?"

"I could tell you knew what was real. I thought any girl who could laugh at the school fashion plate would be someone worth knowing. So I went up and tried to talk to you. Not that you were any help. You said that you were just plain Gwen and I liked that. I could tell everybody looked up to you. The teachers always looked at you when they asked questions. Tony watched after you and Marcia always wanted to talk to you and you wouldn't give her the time of day – "

"You thought I was going to be like Anisha. That's what everybody thought."

"How could I think that when I've never met the girl? You're the one who thinks that. I couldn't care less."

I can see past the trees down to the lake. The wind's blowing the hair out of my face. I pick up a stick and start cracking it into pieces.

"So maybe you're the only one who thinks all anybody notices about you is your glasses."

"But you saw the picture. That is what people notice. Why'd Tony have to draw me like that? I am somebody," she whispers, so I almost can't hear her.

We walk on. She's right beside me, but I feel like I've lost her.

The silence pushes on me. I listen to her breathe. We get to the corner before the school and I reach up to touch her shoulder, but she turns before I get a chance and I whip my hand back behind me.

"Are you staying over tonight, or what?" she says.

"Yeah," I say, and let go a sigh of relief. For a minute I thought that was it, that she would sit beside somebody else and make them be her friend.

"Your dad didn't freak out or anything?" Clara adds snarkily.

"No. Why would he?" So this is what this is about.

"I don't know. He won't let me come over." Her head hangs down again.

"My dad's a private person."

"Because of his art."

Okay. She can think that if she wants.

I'm about to ask Clara why she came to McBurney instead of going back to Central, when we hear the school bell ring. I grab her by the wrist and we make a break for it.

⤙

It's presentation day and we're up next. The last group had the idea of drawing in the walls of the new gym on the construction wall so that everyone could see what it's going to look like when it's finished. They went to the principal's office to get a picture of the new gym to draw from. They made a cardboard model for their presentation so that we could see how the lines in the drawing would line up with the walls of the new building. We were invited to walk around the table to look at it. This guy, Horst, did all the work on his computer so the lines are sharp.

"It's really cool," says Clara in a worried voice.

Tim nudges Tony and goes to flick over the tiny man they put in the model to show where the schoolyard is. Tony grabs Tim's arm.

"Oh, come on," I hear Tim whisper. "If you stand anywhere but right in the middle, the lines don't line up and then it just looks like a bunch of squares." I look at Tony and he's looking straight at me. I can tell he's thinking what I'm thinking. Tim's right. For once. I wonder if anyone else heard him say it. Maybe no one else would notice. Maybe we should say something in our presentation.

I can tell Tony wants to win as badly as I do.

We go back to our seats and Ms. Lenore thanks Horst's group and asks ours to come up.

Clara's set to talk first.

"You've already kind of seen our idea because we chose Gwen's idea of doing superheroes. The idea is that each of us could do a superhero version of ourselves on the construction wall and that will show how the new gym will help us bring out the best we have to offer. We need the new gym to help make us stronger. We can make these pictures show how strong we'll be able to get." Clara sits down and Tim stands up. I'm afraid he's going to say something about the other group's model.

"So we thought that it would be good if everyone made a list of what their superhero powers could be. Like me, for instance," he says, standing up taller. "I could have super hair that grows so fast that it whips straight out of my head and saves people from drowning in the ocean because they could grab onto my hair." Tim stands there waiting, but nobody laughs. I'm afraid we're going to lose it right there. "Fine," says Tim. "You wouldn't think super hair was such a bad power if you were on the *Titanic*." Then everybody laughs. Tim sits down and Tony gets up.

"We didn't make a model," he says, and I go stiff. He's going to ruin it. I can't stand it. "Instead, I made these sketches of the members of my group with their superpowers."

He pulls out the one of Tim as the joker. "This is the one of Tim, but I guess he wants to change to Super Hair Man." Everyone laughs again. Tony is a good artist. He pulls out the picture of Clara. He holds it up and the entire class goes ballistic with laughter. I catch at Clara's hand under the table.

"And this is one of Clara," Tony says over the laughter. He's obviously enjoying himself. It's like

115

the whole idea was his. I'm about to say something when Clara pipes up.

"Of course, I could change my superpower, too," she says.

"Oh, yeah? To what?" says Tim. Clara's face is getting red.

"I'd be Super Make-Hair-Man-Shut-Up Woman." I nearly spit my tongue out at that and so does everyone else. I slap Clara's knee and she turns to me with a grin. Even Tim is laughing. Only Tony doesn't seem to think it's very funny. He's hurt that nobody's looking at his picture anymore. He shuffles around to get the one of me. He turns to the picture of Creative Woman.

"And since it was Gwen's concept, I made her into Creative Woman." The class calms down and you can hear them whispering about the picture. I can feel myself blushing, which makes me blush more. I want to say that I'd change my superpowers, too, but all I can think of is super yellow hands and it would be too hard to explain quickly. Creative Woman sounds pretty good.

It's hard to believe he thinks of me that way. I sneak a peek at the picture again. He pressed hard with the pencil crayon, so you can see he put his energy in it. I can sense power in it, as if it were a picture of someone real. Tony sits down.

I'm up next. I stand up. We have to win.

I focus on Clara, her eyes. Goose bumps. I take a deep breath.

"Tony's pictures show how we can use the idea so that it becomes an idea that belongs to each of us. Also, we think that, like Ms. Lenore said, the community would feel safer with a bunch of super-heroes in the neighborhood. And, since you can choose your own superpowers, it makes you focus on how you could make the world a better place."

I look around at the class and my heart flutters. I lose my train of thought. I'm supposed to say something else but I can't remember what it is. The class is completely quiet. Waiting. I've forgotten something more important. I search my mind for it while they wait. North, East, South, West.

Oh, my God. I didn't do the spell last night.

Somebody coughs. I ruined it. I open my mouth, but nothing comes out. I look down at Tony and then Clara knocks the side of my foot.

I sit down and the class slowly starts clapping. I remember. I forgot to say that thing about self-esteem. That would have sold Ms. Lenore for sure. It's too late. We go back to our seats.

I fell asleep with the postcards on me. They must be in my bed somewhere. Or on the floor. I didn't see them when I got up. I imagine Dad seeing a card on the floor and picking it up, and realizing what it is.

117

I've broken contact for sure. No doubt about me breaking the rules this time.

My eyes well up. Clara touches me on the arm.

"Don't worry. You were good," she lies. I shrug my arm out of her grasp.

"All right," says Ms. Lenore. "We're going to do the democratic thing and take a vote on this. Then I'll present the best idea from this class and the best from the other classes to the principal and one will be chosen." Tim puts up his hand.

"Shouldn't the kids get to choose the final one?" he says. Ms. Lenore glares at him.

"No, Tim."

"That doesn't sound very democratic," Tim says. Then Clara sticks her hand over his mouth and everyone laughs again.

Ms. Lenore passes out the slips for voting. We aren't allowed to vote for our own team so I vote for Horst's group.

"Who'd you vote for?" Tony asks me in the hall after class.

"The group with the model."

"What did you do that for? You should have voted for the worst idea. Think about it, man. Horst's group is our main competition."

My heart sinks. I never thought about that. Clara's slapping her hand against her forehead. "I did that, too."

"Way to go, ladies. What if they win by two votes?" Tim says.

I hate the way Tony thinks he's the leader of our group. I hate it that he's right. I wanted us to win.

The more I want something, the worse my chances are of getting it. I'm a walking jinx.

CHAPTER THIRTEEN

WE'RE ON PATRICK STREET PAST THE park, and I'm running out of time. I can't think of any excuse not to stay over at Clara's. I showed her my overnight stuff in my bag before class this morning, so she knows I didn't forget anything. I can't believe I remembered to pack envelopes of hot chocolate and my toothbrush and then forgot to do the spell. Clara's so excited that I'm coming she won't shut up long enough for me to pretend to get mad at her, so that I can go home and do the spell a few dozen times to make up for forgetting.

"I should warn you about my brother. He wasn't home last time, but he will be tonight because he's grounded. Garth thinks he's too cool to live in a house with a family, so don't take it personally if he ignores you."

We turn the corner onto Raglan.

"My dad's a bit weird, too. He picks the lint out from between his toes while he's watching television. When he's not watching TV, he's in the garage smoking cigars, which Mom won't let him do inside. You didn't meet him before, either, but he's back on day shift. My mom's the most normal, and she still hasn't stopped wearing that suit three times a week. I think she thinks it makes her look thinner. Don't get the wrong idea. She showers every day. Or, at least, when she can get into the bathroom. Garth reeks it up with that cologne. Ever since that girl started calling, you can't go in there without your eyes watering from the smell of it. How many bathrooms does your place have?"

We're coming up to the second turn to her place. I can't think of what to say to get out of this. I *could* make up the spell tomorrow. I mean, if I broke contact and it's ruined, then it can stay ruined for one more night.

Her house is a small house, but you can tell a family lives there from the four bikes on the porch. They are rusted, but you can tell they meant for them to ride together once. And they aren't careful with their stuff. They're messy and they don't worry about it. Not like me. Clara doesn't have to be careful the way I do because her family follows the rules.

You have to be careful if your family doesn't follow the rules because most people can't handle it. Like Mom and Anisha.

Clara's family has no secrets. You can tell that from their house. They leave everything lying out in the open for everybody to see.

"So? How many bathrooms do you have? If I can't go to your house, you could at least tell me about it so I can imagine it," Clara asks in a snarky voice.

"You say anything you want, don't you?" I ask. Clara squints at me.

"Yeah. What does that have to do with how many bathrooms you have?"

"It doesn't. We've got two. One for Dad on the third floor and one for the house — but we kind of treat it like it's mine. I mean, I have to keep it clean. Every Sunday, we clean."

"You have your own bathroom? That is so cool. I wish I could see your house." I put on my warning look. "I know, I know. Maybe your dad will change his mind about having people over."

"I don't think so."

"You'll ask, though? I really want to see it."

"It's a house. Four walls, floors, stairs, rooms. It's no big deal," I say as we go up to her door. I want to go in but she stays on the porch.

"I just want to see it, okay?" she says, almost angry. "You can come to my house any time you like. My parents let me have anyone I want over any time. My family isn't 'ooooh, don't bring anyone over, I might hear them.' We may not have art in my house, and I don't have my own bathroom, but at least my friends are welcome here."

"Okay, okay," I say. "I get your point. Are we going to go in or what? At my house, I'm allowed inside the front door. Geez, Clara." She smiles and turns the doorknob.

"Geez, Gwendoline Isabella."

⁂

We go upstairs to her room, dump our stuff and flop down on the bed. She's cleaned up a bit. There aren't any clothes on the chair and her stuffed animals have been straightened out and put in order from biggest to smallest.

"Here, I want to show you," Clara says. She puts her hands up to her ears. It's like she's been waiting all day to do this. She takes off her glasses and sets them on the bed. Her face is naked without them.

"You look good without them," I say. "I think they are kind of cool, though, because you know who you are, and people who like you know who you are, but it's like they're protection against everyone else, like they can screen out people who think the only beautiful people are supermodels." She fiddles with the glasses, turns them over and pulls at the ends so that I'm afraid she might break them. I wish she would put them back on. Her face isn't right without them. She isn't Clara without them.

I reach for her glasses, but she snatches them away.

"I can't see a thing without them, that's for sure," she says. She puts them back on. "That's better. Wait! Where did you go? Gwen? Gwen?" She's pretending not to see me, groping in the air with both hands. "My glasses must be screening you out."

I dodge behind the door to hide. She has her nightgown hanging on the back of the door. It has a rip in its side. I pull on the doorknob at the back and squeeze the door on myself. The nightgown smushes in my face. She pulls on the other side and a chill of panic runs through me.

It's like when I hid from my mother in the ghost room. She was in the bathroom when I came home from school. I was in grade three then and I was going to surprise her because she had been acting quiet. I went into her closet and kept the door open a crack so I could listen for her. I liked it there, standing behind her clothes with the hems of her dresses brushing against my legs.

Then I heard her on the phone downstairs. I could hear her saying how she couldn't stand it anymore and what was she going to do and how she wanted to get out. I heard her cry and say how she thought she could do it, but that it was too much. She said she had a plan, that she was going to go for a little while, to get things straight in her head. Then it went quiet and I prayed she wouldn't find me. I stood behind her clothes, holding my breath, holding on tight, shivering.

"Okay, Gwen. You win," Clara says. I must have been holding onto her door pretty fiercely. I have a chunk of her nightgown stuck in my mouth, too. How long have I been back here?

I let go of the door handle and let her open it.

"Are you all right?" she asks. "Is something wrong?"

I flop down on her bed. "Why would you think that?"

>-

"And then Clara's mom called us down for dinner. We ate hamburgers and watched this movie about bugs."

"A cartoon?"

"No. Some weird educational thing. I think Clara's mom was trying to impress me. Garth, Clara's brother, was upstairs moping because he's grounded, and he comes down to answer the phone and his mom gives him a dirty look like he's talking too loud and he says, 'No, it's my family putting on the show for my sister's friend.' Then he laughs. I saw Clara's mom pinch Clara's dad to keep him from smirking. The movie was so boring, except did you know female praying mantises eat their boyfriends after sex? And then me and Clara tried to put up the tent in the living room, but it was missing one of the pole thingies, so we ended up pinning a blanket to the sofa and tying the ends to the drapery rod. It was sort of stupid. I mean, we are thirteen, but it's like Clara says. We won't be able to get away with it much longer. We had hot chocolate under there and Garth came down and bugged us, because we were in his way and he wanted to watch television, but we wouldn't let him because it was a democracy and it doesn't matter how big you are in a democracy, you get one vote and there were two of us and one of him." I have to stop to yawn.

"Yeah, and…?" Leon says.

The two of them have been putting me through the grill since I got home. I've been trying to figure out if Leon told Dad about the postcards, but if he did, Dad isn't giving anything away. They're acting like Clara's a rock star or something. They want every single detail.

"That's it. If you think I'm going to tell you what we talked about, you can forget it."

"What did you have for breakfast?" Dad asks.

"Cereal. Shreddies. With brown sugar and fruit punch, or some pink drink. Can I go?"

"I can't believe the brother was grounded and actually stayed home," Leon says. "I'm not satisfied, Kevin. Are you?"

"Yeah, it feels like..." Dad waves his hands in the air as if grabbing for some word.

"Something's missing," says Leon.

I sigh deeply. "Okay, fine. We smoked dope in the basement, knocked back a bottle of whiskey, took off our clothes and ran around the neighborhood naked at three o'clock in the morning. Can I go?"

Dad and Leon read each other's faces.

"I don't see that we can keep her," Dad says to Leon.

"What about the technicality of arriving home late?"

"Nah, she was off by ten minutes. Minor infraction."

"I guess we have to let her go."

They both have these dumb smiles on their faces. I hate them so much.

"Stop looking at me like that. Man, you'd think I'd been to the moon." I get up from the kitchen table and grab my knapsack.

"Sounds like she had a good time," I hear Dad say as I head upstairs.

"Yeah. Nice change, eh?" Leon says.

"She'll have to invite Clara here some time. I'm curious to meet her."

I put the knapsack on the bed and fish through it for the pictures we drew last night. It started off that we were practicing to draw ourselves so that we could make ourselves into superheroes, but then we got to talking and we ended up doing pictures of each other.

Clara was telling me about this girl, Cynthia, who was at canoe camp with her. She's the one who had the big crush on J.W. Reane. She said they were friends for a long time and they still sort of are, like Cynthia sends her letters and stuff. Clara says that Cynthia's parents aren't crazy about the two of them being pen pals. She says she doesn't know why they don't like her, but they don't. Something must have happened at camp. Why didn't she go back to Central? She still hasn't told me.

But I told her everything. I broke Rule Number 1. I told her about the postcards. I had to. She was asking all these questions.

"Who do you think he is?" she asked. I shook my head. "Do you think he's French or Canadian?"

"The postcards are in English."

"Can I see them?" She stopped coloring. I stared at my paper and pressed harder on the purple until the tip went through the paper. I could hear her waiting. I knew that she knew there was something about the postcards because she'd never asked about them. I could tell she was waiting for me to tell her the truth. Not demanding it. Waiting for it.

I sat up and faced her.

"It was my mom who sent me those postcards, Clara. She's my secret admirer…with no return address. I think she's in France. I didn't lie about that. She says she'll send for me, but I don't think she really will. I've been doing this spell to try to make her call, but it isn't working."

"What kind of spell? From a book?" Clara sat up.

"No, I made it up. I use the postcards. I touch each side of each one and say a chant." I told her. I wanted her to know. "Then I make a box out of the postcards and I close my eyes and put myself inside it so I can be with her. I try to feel her writing on the walls of the box. I try to reach out to her with my mind."

"Like mental telepathy." Clara nodded and reached for a blue crayon. We colored in silence for a bit. I could hear Clara holding her breath.

"It's good she sent the postcards. At least you know she still thinks about you," she said.

My heart flipped like a fish out of water. I couldn't look at her. I put my head down on my picture. I guess I fell asleep then.

⋋

I listen for Dad and Leon at my bedroom door. They're in the TV room. I lie on the bed and place the postcards in a stack, writing side down, on my forehead.

Dear Mom,

This is your daughter. I'm talking straight from my head so you won't have to hide this letter from your boyfriend. I couldn't send you a letter if I wanted to because I don't know where you live. I know you think about me. I know you think I'm a year younger than I am. I know it's hard to remember because it's been so long. I can hardly remember you. What I do remember is you saying on the phone that you couldn't take it anymore and what I need to know is, did you mean me?

I have a best friend again. Her name is Clara. She's crazy. If I come to see you…whenever…I'm trying not to let bad thoughts get in the way of this brain message to you, but I'm not sure I'm doing it right.

Can you hear me? Send me a sign if you can.

Your biological daughter,
Gwendoline Bainbridge

I lie in bed waiting for the sign.

CHAPTER FOURTEEN

CLARA'S FAMILY GOES TO CHURCH ON Sunday. It shouldn't seem like such a weird thing to do, except that it's weird to think that's where she is when I'm getting up at 11:21. I can smell coffee and bacon. I feel so warm and lazy under the covers that I could lie here forever smelling the air with my cold nose.

I don't know if I believe in God. I believe in something. I'm not sure what It is. And I don't know how to show whatever It is that I do believe. I pull my arms from the covers and stretch them toward the window and shoot rays of belief out the ends of my fingers.

I take a deep breath. Mmmm. I believe in bacon.

I catch the sound of Leon's voice downstairs. I can't hear what he's saying, but it sounds serious. I listen more closely and hear Dad ask a question. Can't make it out. I carefully lower my feet to the floor and make my way to the door. At first there's nothing, but then someone puts a coffee cup on the table.

"She might be all right with it," Leon says. "Kids are so resilient...and it's not like I'm a stranger." They're talking about me.

"She's hardly a child anymore. She'll be out of here before we know it," says Dad.

Did Leon tell him about the postcards? I hold my breath.

"What if she fights with me the whole time? I don't want it to be like that. It hasn't exactly been bliss for me, either. I love her to death, but she won't let me in. Whenever we begin to connect, she turns on me."

"Be fair, Leon," Dad says. "How would you feel?"

"God, Kevin, are we ready for this?"

I open the door wider and it creaks. I listen again, but they've stopped talking. They heard me, so I have to go downstairs.

I wander into the kitchen trying to appear sleepy and like I haven't heard anything. They try to act casual in their bathrobes. Then Dad smiles like he has something to tell me.

"Leon's going to move in here, isn't he?" I say.

Nobody says anything. I start shaking my head.

"You didn't ask me. When were you going to tell me?"

Dad goes to open his mouth in that stuttering way he has where his lips flap together but nothing comes out. I imitate him to his face and he stops. I turn to give Leon the evil eye, but he's already got his fierce squint on. It scares me. He hates it when I imitate Dad.

I run upstairs and lock myself in the bathroom. I catch myself in the mirror.

"She might be all right with it," I mouth. As if I had a choice. The ends of my mouth aim for the floor like two daggers. I hop in the tub and draw the curtain across.

I turn on the tap with my foot and let the warm water soak my pajamas. I peel them off and lower my head under the water. All I can hear is the rush.

༝

The doorbell wakes me up. I slosh sideways in the tub. The water's cold. How long have I been in here? I stand up and grab a towel. My skin is covered in goosebumps. My teeth chatter as I step out of the tub.

Behind me there's a knock at the door. I'm so cold.

"Gwen?" It's Dad. This is so stupid. It's not like I can live in here. I sit on the floor between the toilet and the tub and pull another towel over my legs. "You've been in there long enough, Gwen... Gwen?" He jiggles the handle.

"What?"

"This isn't solving anything. Come on out, lovey."

"I'll come out if you go away."

"Oh, come on! Open the door so we can talk. I'm tired of these games, Gwen."

"I'm naked, Dad. I took a bath. I want to go to my room and put something on, okay?" I can hear him thinking about it.

"Okay. Come downstairs after." I wait until I hear him on the stairs and then I run for my bedroom. I put on my jeans with the hole in the knee and my blue hooded sweatshirt, but I'm still cold. I want to climb into bed. The clock reads 1:38. I was in there for more than two hours.

When I get down to the kitchen, Leon stands up and opens his arms to hug me with this big, apologetic, goofy face. I almost laugh at him, but then I push him away.

"What's he doing here?" I say to Dad.

"Gwen!" Dad yells.

"Come on, Kevin. Let her get it out of her system."

"This isn't going to get out of my system," I scream. "You guys think you can rearrange my whole life and I don't get to say anything about it?"

"We are not rearranging your life," Dad says.

134

"If he moves in here, that's a pretty big rearrangement."

"You know it's not," says Leon. "And you know I love you."

"That's supposed to make it okay to ruin my life?"

Dad gets up. "Leon is part of this family."

"Since when?" I say. "Why wasn't I notified?"

I've never seen Dad's face so red. He comes toward me and I shrink back. I'm afraid he's going to hit me. He flaps his mouth and I go to imitate him, but then he whispers so calmly it's like he's talking to my veins.

"Since you know exactly when."

"No, I don't. Since he moved his office here? When?" Dad waits. "When he started sleeping over? I don't remember being asked about that, either." I hear my crushed-glass voice as if it is coming out of someone else.

"We talked about that," Dad whispers. "You remember, Gwen. I asked you — "

"'Do you know what gay is?' Yeah, that's really a talk, Dad."

"There was more to it and you know it."

"You keep telling me I know this stuff. You never said what you — "

"Come on, Gwen. You're a smart girl. You can pretend all you want not to know. Maybe that's

135

easiest for you. But it's time, Gwen. It was wrong of me to go about it like we were embarrassed." He walks over toward Leon and takes his hand.

"No. No. No. *NO. NO.*" They're holding hands and it looks right, but I don't want it to be like that. I clap my hands over my eyes. Dad comes over and pries them off.

"Come on, lovey. It's all right. We're not going to ignore it anymore. It'll be better," he says.

"Kevin," Leon says softly. "We don't absolutely have to do this."

"Yes, we do," Dad says, running a hand over my head. "It's been long enough and Gwen has to understand. We can't keep catering to this ridiculous shame." He says it like he's been practicing. What comes next comes out so strong. "I want to be out. I want for Gwen to be out."

"But I don't want that," I cry, and it's like I've slapped him across the face.

"When do you think you'll be ready?" Dad hisses.

"*NEVER!* I want him to go. I hate him. He can't stay here."

Leon's crying. I run into him and push him toward the door. "I don't want you. Go away. *NOW.* Go." He moves backwards, but Dad catches both my wrists and holds them tight.

"It's not him you're mad at, Gwen."

"Yes, it is. I hate him. He's the one who made her leave and I'll hate him forever."

Dad and Leon look at each other and it makes me burst into tears.

I'm never going to France. She's never coming back. I'm never going to see her.

Dad folds my arms back and pushes me into a chair.

"This is about her. You don't want to give up on her yet, do you?"

"Who?" I say. I'm shaking. Tears fall faster than I can wipe them away. In five years, he hasn't said her name. I'm making him say it.

"Your mother."

I whip my head toward Leon.

"You told?"

He shakes his head, scared. Dad's lips are fluttering. I knock my head into his chest and something in me falls away. A curse, a spell. Dad's arms close around me and then Leon's arms close around us both.

⪼

Anisha acted stunned when I told her about Dad. We were sitting on top of the picnic table in Skeleton Park. It was August and you could see waves of heat rising off the asphalt. I thought, she's my best friend, she's leaving for Ottawa soon, she should know everything. She's earned it.

137

That's what I seriously thought. I thought she'd understand, and it would be this great bond between us and we could write to each other about it.

It went the opposite way.

First, it took ten minutes to explain it to her because she didn't believe that gay men could have children. Then her perfect face went screwy. For once she didn't seem to be concerned that her mascara might smudge.

"Ew. Ewwww. Oh, my God. I never heard of that before. Did you inherit it?" she asked. She looked like I was going to jump her right there.

"Come on. It's not like that and you know it."

"Are you sure?" she said, turning her legs away from me and clutching her elbows into her sides. I hated the way she was looking at me in her stupid low-cut plaid blouse and tight jean shorts and that useless makeup on her perfect brown skin, with the sides of her hair flipped back.

At that moment, everything that used to impress me about her revolted me.

I leaned over and tried to kiss her. She turned her face and I got her on the ear. She slapped her hand over it and flew back like I was trying to kill her. Her hand was shaking.

I started laughing my head off.

"You've got the cooties," I said. I half expected

her to join in with me, to see the joke of the whole thing, but she didn't.

"Stay away from me," she said. "Don't ever touch me again." Then she walked away from me, rubbing her ear like she had just pulled a leech off it.

CHAPTER FIFTEEN

CLARA IS STANDING ON THE CORNER WAIT-ing for me with the picture I drew of her in her hand. She's smiling with her whole face, like she can't wait to show everybody what great friends we are. I grab the piece of paper out of her hand as I meet her at the corner. I make a show out of rolling it up.

"Hello, Marcia?" I say, putting the roll to my ear. Clara thinks I'm hilarious. "You know how I said that Clara was going to be the most popular girl in school this year? Well, that's only because her tits are bigger than yours." I crush the picture into Clara's stunned face, but she doesn't lift her hands to take it. So I drop it and it blows down the sidewalk like a piece of trash.

Clara winces. Her big x-ray eyes fog over and drip, but it's like something that is happening far away or on TV.

"Why?" she whines. I turn away and keep walking. I listen for her footsteps behind me, but I can't make them out.

Good. I got rid of her. It was easier than I thought. I stop at the corner and listen, but all I hear is the scraping of leaves against the street.

There's no way I can have Clara for a friend now. Not with her goody-two-shoes, play-by-the-rules, go-to-church family. She'd never understand.

I'm a loner again. I knew that was the smart thing to do.

Clara's still standing in the middle of the sidewalk, wiping her face. Oh, boo-hoo. I can't believe she was going to bring that picture to school. God. I mean, things like that between friends, that stuff is supposed to be private.

Being a loner is the right way to be because nobody knows me – not the whole, full, true me. People like it better when everyone fakes that everything in their lives is perfect – like they've all jumped out of one of those Christmas card photographs of a smiling family in matching clothes. People don't know what to do with the whole truth. They leave.

I'm tired of faking it with fakers.

Dear Mother,

Thanks for leaving me alone in this world full of crap artists and fake friends.

Wait. That's not right.

Dear Mother,

I hope you are enjoying your fake normal life. My life sucks, but at least it's real. I am now telepathically giving you the finger.

⤞

Ms. Lenore announces the winner of the mural vote in art class. Our group won. Clara turns to me with this pleading, confused face. My throat tightens. I stare straight ahead to block her out. Anyway, it still has to be approved by the principal. It's not like my mother would care about something so stunned and little as the mural contest. I can imagine what she would say if I won the Nobel Prize for science. *Dear Gwen, Did I hear you did well in science class or something? Good for you. Maybe one of these days you'll be a real scientist. Have you ever tasted goat cheese? I'm in Greece now...*

This is what loners do. They make up nasty letters in their heads addressed to the relatives who abandoned them and made it impossible for them to have any friends.

Tony and Tim come up to me in the hall after class.

"Hey, we won," says Tony.

I keep walking. Tim double-steps up beside me.

"Did you and Super Shut-Up-Hair-Guy Girl get into a fight or something?" he asks.

142

"It's none of your business, Tim."

"It is too our business," says Tony, adjusting his knapsack on his shoulder. "We're a group, remember? We're supposed to be working together. If they pick our idea, then we're going to be in charge of the whole thing. We'll be the directors of the mural." I can tell he's been having little director fantasies about ordering kids around while they're trying to paint the stupid construction wall. That used to be what I wanted, too. I imagined the four of us wearing hard hats, and Clara getting paint on her leg, and Tim putting more paint on Clara's leg, and Tony picking up a little kid so she can paint near the top, and me helping Tony with the kid.

Another bubblegum fantasy popped. C'est la vie.

"Just because we're in the same group doesn't mean we have to like each other, Tony," I say with a fixed sneer. Tim pulls on his friend's arm.

"Come on, Tony. I think she's PMS."

I watch them make their way down the hall.

I get my humungazoid sandwich from my desk and head for the lunch room. As I walk through the glass doors I can tell something's wrong. Marcia is sitting in my chair across from Clara, laughing her head off. Clara stares straight at me, holding her breath.

143

I have to change things forever and for good. I know what I have to do.

The lunch room doors close, making a breeze at my back that pushes me farther into the room. Marcia's giving me the once-over, from tip to toe and back again.

I keep moving toward the empty seat I'm aiming for. I pass inches away from Tony and Tim at their corner table. The last few steps seem to take a million years. I can hear my breath inside my head.

"Is this seat taken?" I ask. J.W. Reane shrugs.

The lunch room ceiling has 280 tiles. I counted. Tomorrow, I start on the holes in the tiles.

❧

I'm polite at dinner. Dad says Leon will move in October 1.

"Fine," I say. I don't look at them. I look at their hands cutting their pork chops. Leon heaps the mustard on. Dad takes smaller bites. When they start talking about where to put Leon's stuff, I ask to be excused. I quietly pick up my dishes, take them to the kitchen and wash them, so they have no reason to talk to me.

I'm too tired to talk. My head feels like a cannonball.

I lie on my bed, fold my arms across my eyes.

My mother ran away because she couldn't face

144

it about Dad and Leon. I didn't have a choice. Neither did Dad. I guess he could have gone on pretending that he was straight, but it would have been a lie. It would have been a nice lie for me. I could have friends over and not have to worry about them gawking at Leon and my gay dad, giggling at how they are together, joking about what they do in bed at night. That's what they'd think about if they knew the truth. It's what I used to think about.

Why couldn't Dad and Leon have lied for me?

People still don't look at a gay person the same way they look at a straight one. Maybe Dad doesn't care about that anymore, but I do. I don't want people looking at him thinking that's what his whole life is about.

It shouldn't be that way, but it is. Why do we have to be the ones who change it? Why couldn't it already be changed, so that I could be normal?

I told Anisha that it was Dad who did the portraits. I said he used photographs to make them. It was a lie. I thought she'd catch it for sure. Instead, it turned out to be the one thing I told her that truly impressed her. She really admired those portraits. I can hardly stand to look at them.

We sat for the first portrait in the backyard, by the sunflowers. Mom said she wanted us to be free and natural. She wore jeans, Dad wore a baseball cap and I wore my best green velvet dress. Mom wanted me to go upstairs and change into something less formal, but Leon said we were perfect and started drawing. The portrait shows exactly what Leon saw then. Mom's tight mouth, Dad's stiff arm around her and me sitting crosslegged between them happy as a clam, thinking this meant we were a real family again, like before Mom moved out of Dad's room and into the ghost room.

Then Dad called Leon back to do another portrait of me and him for Mom for Christmas. It was a secret. I was so excited. I kidded around with Leon the whole time. We played I Spy. We were on the couch in the living room this time. Leon kept choosing things that were behind me but when I'd turn my head to look he'd say, 'Look this way. Don't move.' It ended up he didn't do one of me and Dad, he did three. I'm laughing in one, trying to keep a straight face in another and perfectly bored in the third.

Mom called Leon back the third time to do portraits of me and her to match the ones of me and Dad. That was her mistake. We did that one in the kitchen with Mom on one side of the table and me on the other. Dad sat beside Leon while he sketched and you can see from the way it turned out how much Mom hated every minute of it. There were supposed to be three pictures again, but Mom said she was happy with just the one.

She couldn't have been happy with that one. Leon made her look so sour and cramped between the table and the kitchen sink.

And there I am across the table, smiling like an idiot, oblivious to what was going on right in front of me. Mom saw, though. I can see it in her painted eyes. She knew Dad and Leon were falling in love.

CHAPTER SIXTEEN

THICK FOG. CAN'T SEE THE BACKYARD fence from the kitchen window. Leon comes in, still in his bathrobe with the little green race cars.

"Morning," he says.

"How can you tell?"

"Are you going to be angry at me the rest of your life?" He takes a cup from the cupboard, pours himself some coffee and leans against the counter. Dad has already gone to work.

I take my dishes and put them in the sink. Leon's waiting for an answer.

"Okay, you can be mad at me if you want," he says. "As long as it's therapeutic." Then I have to listen to him take a sip of coffee. I can hear it slither through his teeth. I grab an apple from the bowl on the table and take off.

I like fog. The way it blurs the edges of everything and makes it so no one can see you. I breathe it in, let the mist comb my face. A blotch in the distance comes slowly into focus.

Clara's waiting for me at the corner.

I can't believe it. I cross the street. She crosses, too, and walks toward me, holding her head up, chin jutting forward. I grind my teeth, passing her, and catch the smell of Garth's cologne hanging in the damp air as I walk by. It chokes the back of my throat.

"I don't know what's gotten into you, Gwen. But you aren't getting rid of me that easily." I start running to get out of this circle of fog that holds the two of us together. The blur of the purple slash on my white sneakers eats up the wet pavement. I slow down when I hit the park to avoid skidding on the soggy leaves covering the path. I reach the pile of rocks and mortar that marks the middle of Skeleton Park, where the paths cross.

I start toward the left, but it's too late. Clara's got me. She yanks on the back of my knapsack and I throw myself against the rocks, bringing her full weight against me.

"Get off me," I gasp. She tries to get me by the shoulders. "Stop it. Leave me alone, you fat, bubble-eyed geek."

She lets go and I take off again, speeding into the gray with everything I've got.

I reach school out of breath and hit the washroom. I'm warm and wet. The mirror shows my

149

eyes, too big and surprised, and my chin, too small and pointy. I lean across the counter and breathe a cloud against it. That's better. I'm foggy. I'm almost invisible.

I try to stay invisible in class, but every time I forget and sneak a look at Clara, she winks and mouths the word "later," like she's planning to beat me up after school. And suddenly she's everyone's favorite person. I go to the lunch room and Tony, Tim and Marcia are sitting with Clara at our old table, laughing like they are all best buddies — like *I* was the one keeping them apart all this time.

I know I'm failing at being invisible when I walk down the middle aisle of the lunch room. All eyes are on me.

I go to sit with J.W. again. He puts both arms around his sandwich and pulls it toward him.

"I hope you don't mind me sitting here," I whisper. He looks at his food and shrugs. He's got one of his truck T-shirts on. I try to imagine him as one of the most popular boys at St. Matthew's Camp, but it's a stretch.

"Clara told me you guys went to camp together," I say.

I want J.W. to talk to me so that at least I won't have to think about those guys watching me not talking to J.W., which would be worse, somehow. I want to show them I mean to be sitting at the loner table.

I turn back to J.W. He's got egg salad on his cheek. I clear my throat.

"She tells me you are a hotshot canoeist."

He raises his eyebrows.

"Paddling's not rocket science." His voice is deeper than I remember. He's staring at his lunch.

"She said this girl, Cynthia, had a crush on you," I say. He shakes his head.

"That's not true." He puts his sandwich down and wipes his arm across his face.

He's not un-handsome. He's got nice hands. He's got pen marks on the inside of his elbow. He never takes off that stupid yellow sun hat.

I try to imagine he's cute. But he's J.W. He's been J.W. for so long, it's hard to imagine him as anyone else. In my head he's still the kid who threw up on the teacher's desk in grade five. I can't get past the drooling-on-the-arm thing.

"I heard your aunt brought you up," I say. His gaze travels up to the ceiling.

"If you want to sit here, fine. But don't pretend you like me, because I know you don't. You haven't said anything to me since that time in kindergarten."

It whips out of him, like he's been storing it up.

It hits me that every day for years he's been J.W. Reane, king geek, and nobody talked to him. Not me, either.

"I'm sorry." I try to concentrate on my food and not think of anything.

I can feel those guys looking over at me and him, noticing the angry look on J.W.'s face. Every clanky sound in the lunch room twitches the hairs on the back of my neck. I sniff and try to suck it back in, but it's too late already. I cup my hand over the front of my face.

I hear J.W. whisper to himself. "This is the way it had to go, didn't it?" I hear him sigh and mutter, "First time a girl talks to you at school and you make her cry. That's bliming wonderful. Okay, don't worry about it. I'll go outside." He starts piling things into his knapsack and I grab his milk.

"Don't. I mean, I'm sorry."

He moves his eyes quickly to the ceiling. I reach over and push down on his knapsack and he sits down with it.

"Tell me what I said to you in kindergarten," I ask. Finally, he looks at me.

"You said, 'J.W., you are a strange salad eater and pork friend.'"

"What?" He nods.

"I brought a head of lettuce to school for show and tell. It was from our garden. I must have talked

152

about my uncle's pig farm up near Enterprise, too. I remember because it was the only time I ever brought in anything for show and tell and you were the only one who said anything." He takes a deep breath.

"And I said you were a strange salad eater and pork friend?"

"Yes." He takes another bite of his egg salad sandwich.

"Well...don't you think that was friendly?" I say. Crumbs come sputtering out of the sides of his mouth and he has to cup his hand over his face to not lose his whole mouthful.

J.W. is laughing. I can't tell whether it's real or fake. I don't think I've ever heard him laugh before. It sounds like he's choking.

He shakes his head and begins to quiet down, eyeing Clara's table.

"Clara's nice," he says.

"Yeah, she is. That's kind of the problem," I say.

"Why?"

"It just is."

"She didn't tell you about the other thing?" he says, shooting a quick look at me before directing his gaze once again to his good friend, the ceiling.

"What other thing?"

He looks over at the other table and shakes his head.

153

I look behind me and catch Clara looking in our direction again. I keep my eyes on her and wait for her to mouth the word "later." But instead, she blushes so fiercely, I swear I can feel the heat coming off her face.

❧

I rush out of school right at the bell and start running. I keep going until I hit Division and then I slow down to a walk. I wander around looking at the houses. Some are brick, but most have vinyl siding. Most of them are two stories, like Clara's, but not one is the exact same height as the one next to it. I imagine the families who live in them, sitting in their living rooms watching television, eating microwave popcorn and arguing over the remote.

I have to stop for a car backing out of a driveway. When I realize where I am, I walk half a block more and stop. Between the houses in front of me, I can see Clara's backyard. I climb over the wire garden fence into the backyard backing onto Clara's.

I want to see if she invited Marcia over.

I make a spot for myself in the bushes and sit down on my knapsack. Clara's house is quiet.

I'm about to leave when I see Mr. Scanlan come out the back door. I go still. He walks over to the garage and sits on the stoop. He pulls a cigar and a lighter from his front shirt pocket and lights up. The smell of it drifts toward me.

The back screen door squeaks open and Garth leans out and says something.

"Now?" his father says. Garth nods. Mr. Scanlan rests his cigar on the stoop, gets up and goes into the house. Garth goes over, picks up the cigar and takes a huge puff. I can tell he's done it before. He watches the back of the house, takes another drag and replaces it on the stoop one second before Mr. Scanlan comes out. Mr. Scanlan walks over to him and pokes him in the cheek. Smoke sputters out of Garth's mouth.

"You think I'm going to let you do that? Eh, punk? Your mother would kill us both. Here." He passes the cigar back to Garth, who takes a drag. "Okay. Go help your sister with her math."

"She asked for you," Garth says.

"Yeah, but I forgot that stuff already and you did it a couple of years ago, so you help her."

"I'm going to tell Mom you can't do grade eight math," Garth says.

"Yeah, well...go ahead. And be nice to your sister. She's upset."

"She's always upset," says Garth, moving toward the back door.

"Yeah, and you're always grounded," replies Mr. Scanlan, making his way back down to the stoop.

"And you're always in the dog house," says Garth.

"Hell in a handbasket," they say at the same time and laugh.

"Better make it a four-door handbasket, eh, Garth?"

"What? Grandma's not coming? Better make it a mini-van," he says and goes inside.

Then it's Mr. Scanlan smoking his cigar. A light goes on in the kitchen. I can see Clara. She goes to the fridge and takes out a piece of bread and some bologna. She folds the meat inside the bread and takes a huge bite. She walks over to the garbage can and throws the uneaten portion away. Then she spits her mouthful on top of it. Her brother walks in, opens the garbage and says something to Clara. She yells something back at him and storms out of the room.

Garth opens the back door and leans out.

"She's doing it again, Dad." Mr. Scanlan stubs out his cigar and goes inside.

Then, that's it. Whatever's going on, I can't see it from here.

A young woman in shorts sitting on the front porch watches me walk out of her backyard. I take off. I run all the way home with one line repeating itself in my head.

"Clara needs me."

CHAPTER SEVENTEEN

I HAVE TO WAIT FOR ALMOST AN HOUR before Leon's off the phone. I pace between the TV room and the ghost room, going over what I could say to Clara. "I made a mistake. I didn't mean to hurt you."

But that's not true. I have to say what's true. I have to tell her everything. I have to fix this.

The second Leon clicks off, I rip the phone out of his hand and run for the bathroom.

I sit in the bathtub, clear my throat and dial Clara's number. Garth answers.

"Is Clara there?"

"Yeah, hold on." I can hear him drop the phone on the table and walk to the kitchen. Then there are voices in the background. I hear Garth say, "You ask her who she is." Then footsteps and a breath.

"Who's calling, please?" It's Mr. Scanlan's voice.

"It's Gwendoline Bainbridge." I hear more muffled voices. He must have his hand over the mouthpiece. I brace my feet against the end of the tub.

"I'm sorry, Gwen. Clara doesn't want to talk to you," he says.

I can't speak. There's a knock on the bathroom door.

"All right," I say to the phone. Another knock at the door.

"I wish you girls wouldn't fight. It's upsetting," Mr. Scanlan says. Knock.

"I know," I sputter. I lower the phone to my lap and press the Talk button to hang up.

Another tap on the door. I step out of the tub and whip the door open.

Dad's standing there looking all concerned.

I hand him the phone and head past him to my room.

He follows me in and closes the door. I take one look at him and his lop-sided grin and burst.

He sits down beside me and wipes my tears with his thumbs. "What's this about?"

"I'm so mean. I'm so bad," I say.

"Is this about Leon moving in?" I shake my head. "It is, isn't it?" He takes me by the shoulders. "I knew this might be hard. If it's too much for you, we can figure something out. He can stay

158

at his place until you've had a chance to – "

"That's not it, Dad. I made a mistake. I was so mean to her. She only wanted to be my friend and now she won't talk to me."

"Clara? What happened?"

I get up and walk to the desk to get the picture Clara drew of me. I pull it out of the drawer. Underneath it are the postcards. The last one is on top. *Maybe Christmas, huh?*

I pull them out and hold them to my chest.

Dad's sitting there, waiting.

I walk back over to the bed and drop the whole mess in front of him. He picks up the picture and smiles. Then he reaches for a postcard.

He reads postcard number four.

"When did you get these?"

"Over the summer." He flips through the others.

"Do they say where she is?" I shake my head.

Dad starts pacing the room. He's still in his crisp work clothes. His black shoes crack against the wood floor. His eyes dart around the room, out the window, out the door, to the bed and back to me.

He reads another one, then another one, shaking his head the whole time. He takes a deep breath before turning back to me.

"Did she call? That's it, isn't it? You think you said something mean? What could you have said that's worse than what she did to you? You have a right to be angry. Five years with nothing and now — " He holds up the postcards with shaky hands.

"No, Dad. I know that," I scream. We are both trembling. "I'm not stupid. I know she doesn't want me." He walks toward me, but I back away from him. "She won't call. I know that. And I am angry at her, okay? But that's not it."

I shove the postcards aside and sit on the bed. "It's about Clara. I was so mean to her. I ruined her picture. I threw it on the street. She was so nice to me. She took me to her house and she has everything. I wanted her to feel as bad as me and it worked. She told her dad she doesn't want to talk to me." I squeeze the words out of my clenched throat.

"Why? What do you mean she has everything?"

"She has a mother."

Dad grabs me and holds on tight.

➤

She's waiting for me at the corner again. My heart hops to see her there. I try to check her eyes from half a block away. I walk toward her. I can't help smiling.

She turns her back on me and starts walking.

"I'm sorry, Clara," I call. She keeps walking. I have to run to catch up. I take her by the elbow, but she shakes me off and keeps walking.

"I was horrible. You have every right to be mad." I pull the picture out of my knapsack. I run in front of her and wave it in her face.

"Here, take it. I did it for you." She tries to walk around me, but I won't let her. I unroll the picture and hold it in front of her face. Her fingertips appear on the edge of the paper and I release it into her hands.

"I worked on it all night after dinner. I'm sorry, Clara."

Some of the red pastel I used for the dress has rubbed off onto her thumb.

"This is me?" she says, lifting her eyes to mine.

"Yeah. I've seen you singing on the corner. I thought it could be your superhero thing." I can't tell whether she likes it or not. "Maybe when you sing, everybody stops what they're doing and listens." I swallow hard and watch her hands to see if they are going to do what mine did and crumple the thing up.

"Why were you so angry at me?" she asks, still staring at the picture I drew of her, singing, with her arms wide open, in a long, red dress.

"I wasn't angry. I think I was scared." The wind rustles the paper in her hands.

"Why?"

I promised myself I'd tell her the truth. It's like pulling at a sliver to get it out. I take a deep breath.

161

"I was scared you would end up being like Anisha."

"I'm nothing like her. Wasn't she supposed to be beautiful?"

"She was supposed to be a lot of things she wasn't. She was supposed to be my best friend, but she couldn't take being a real friend. She didn't want to know the real me. She never *asked* about my mom. And I had her over to my place, but she never asked to come see my house. She wanted me to be her friend, but she wasn't interested in me. Not like you."

Clara rolls her eyes and starts walking again, holding the picture between two fingers like it is a snotty tissue.

My heart drops to my stomach. It pounds there.

I can hear her runners squeak against the sidewalk with every step she takes.

It's my turn to be the one who makes the other one be her friend.

I catch up to her and tug on her arm to make her stop. I catch her x-ray eyes. I can see how much I hurt her and she sees that I see. She breaks and looks down at the picture. She stands there for the longest time, staring at it. I can hear her breathing – short angry breaths at first, and then longer, deeper ones. I reach for her with my mind. I send her my full mental sorry. I'm still sending when she looks up again.

"I thought maybe I did something, maybe I said something. I was going crazy trying to figure it out. I was going to beat you up to find out," she says.

"You were not."

"Sure I was. I was going to knock you down and sit on you until you talked. Tim was going to sit on your feet." She rolls up the picture and we start walking.

"So that means he'd be sitting beside you, right?" I tease.

"Do you want me to forgive you or not?"

I grab her arm and loop it through mine.

⤞

Walking into the lunch room, I whisper to Clara that we should sit with J.W.

"I don't want to," she says. I can see her looking toward our old table where Marcia, Tony and Tim are waiting. She gives a little wave to Marcia, who waves back at her and throws me a smile so cold and fake, I swear I can hear ice cracking off her teeth.

I start heading in the direction of J.W.'s table.

"*NOOO,*" Clara says so loudly that everything goes quiet in the lunch room. She puts her hands over her glasses, leans forward and marches down the aisle toward the door. When she bangs into it, she stops, turns around and pushes it open with her bum. Then she starts running.

I take off after her. My heart grows fatter in my chest as I jog down the hall. I see myself in my mind running down the hall after my best friend. I see my legs kicking, my arms pumping, the look on my face.

I land at the washroom door and push it open.

I find the stall with her feet in it and push at the door. It opens and there she is sitting on the toilet with her pants still up. She's panting. She looks sick.

"Leave me alone."

"I can't," I say.

"You think you can apologize and we'll just be friends again? But it has to be all your way because you're the pretty one, right? You're right that I'm not like Anisha. I've never been popular. Nobody likes a fat girl."

"You aren't fat."

"You think you're so smart, but you don't know anything about me." She crosses her arms and turns her head into the wall.

"If you talked to me, then I would know you...dear," I tell her. I can tell she remembers saying it to me that time we had the pillow fight at her house. She sits perfectly still and stares at me through narrowed eyes.

The light in the room seems to dim and the air comes alive with small sounds — the shifting of Clara's shirt, the hum of the fluorescent lights, me trying to swallow the sudden lump in my throat.

Clara starts speaking. Her voice is low, so that I have to lean into the stall to hear her.

"I was a junior counselor this summer. The kids liked me. But the other junior counselors... Cynthia was nice. She came from Cornwall. Her uncle is the minister at my church and her parents were having some problems so she got sent to live here for the summer. So there was me, Cynthia, J.W., and these guys Martin and Andy. Those two were complete jerks.

"Last year, I grew a lot. A real lot. And not up, but out. At camp we wore bathing suits all the time, so you can imagine what those jerks said. Martin and Andy called me Clorca, like a killer whale. Stuff like that and also about my chest. They'd walk behind me and Martin would make a swishing sound, which was supposed to be my thighs rubbing together, and Andy would go 'boompa, boompa,' which was supposed to be my boobs going up and down. At first I ignored them. But they kept going. Then I yelled at them, but they kept on and on and on. The older counselors told them off, but that was even more embarrassing. It was Cynthia — "

"What happened?"

She takes a deep breath. "She told me that she used to be fat but that she had this way of keeping thin and she showed me what she did in the washroom at the camp."

"What?"

"You know," she says and sticks two fingers in her mouth. Oh. "Throw up. She said she had girlfriends in Cornwall who showed her how and that she got a boyfriend after she skinnied up. He told her to do it. They'd eat at McDonald's and he'd say, 'Time for the ladies' room, Cyn.' Nice, eh? I think that's why she liked J.W. so much, because he was the exact opposite of her boyfriend. She was doing it, so it didn't seem so bad. I knew those guys weren't going to stop teasing me so I started doing it, too."

"Oh, Clara."

"It sounds disgusting, but it got to feel normal. I felt like I could do anything I wanted. I could eat anything and it wouldn't matter. Afterwards, I'd feel clean. Those guys would tease me, but what they said didn't bother me so much anymore. They must have been able to tell, because they stopped. The whole thing felt like I'd found this secret way to make everything go right. I started losing weight. Sometimes I still can't see what was so wrong about it. I'd probably still be doing it, if I didn't get caught."

"A counselor caught you?" I say.

"No. It was the birthday of this one kid, and her mom had baked a cake. You wouldn't believe the size of this cake. The mother was there, too, video-taping us eating cake. I think I had three pieces. After, Cynthia and I went up to the washroom to throw up. So I'm bent over the toilet and I hear this 'zzzzoom' sound. I look up and there's Martin hanging over the top of the stall with the camcorder. I think he thought he was going to get us naked, changing into our bathing suits. You could tell what I was doing from the tape. I still had my fingers in my mouth when I looked up. Martin didn't say anything. He left."

I can almost picture the video in my head. There's everybody outside in the park eating cake and having a good time. And then there's Clara, bent over a toilet, throwing it up.

"Mom says I'm lucky the lady recognized me from the tape. She says that lady saved my life by going to them with it. God, you never want your parents to find out about something like that. Mom — it was like I'd hit her. The lady told the minister at my church, too, so we had to go in and talk to him. Then he wanted my whole family to come in."

I squinch into the stall beside her and put my arm around her shoulders.

"Martin and Andy told everyone from school. A couple of girls called to say how sorry they felt for me. And one of them was this girl, Julia. Ms. Popularity. She said, 'I didn't think you were that fat, Clara. Honest.' That's when I told Mom I wanted to go to McBurney. How could I go back to Central knowing how they'd look at me?" She bites her lip and I feel a stretch in my arm as she sighs beneath it.

"It didn't exactly feel wrong. It felt like a way of trying to make things go right. Like what you did with the postcards. It was my spell. When I went to do it, it was like you said. I'd go into a box and I'd do it in the box and it'd be safe there, but it wasn't real. In the box, it was like I was watching a video of me doing it, only the girl on the video couldn't be me. Mom said maybe we should take me to see a psychologist."

"Do you want to?" I ask. Clara shakes her bowed head and puts one hand over her eyes.

"When I think about it, it's so embarrassing. I see that video in my brain and I want it to just stop there. I want to be normal. I'm pretty sure…I think I'm all right. Last night, Garth caught me spitting food in the garbage, but I was just upset because you were mad at me. That's what I told Mom. I told her about what you did with wrecking the picture and sitting with J.W., and she said it sounded like you probably had problems of your own. Show's how much she knows, eh?" Clara's voice finally cracks. When she huffs to try to catch back the tears, I can smell mint gum on her breath.

I cringe with deep-down sorriness. I lift Clara's hand and rub her knuckles against my cheek. She's staring at the floor. I can tell she doesn't want to look at me, but I have to make her.

I squeeze her hand so hard that she has to look up.

"Do you want to come over to my place tonight?" I ask.

CHAPTER EIGHTEEN

ON THE WAY HOME TO MY HOUSE, CLARA'S going on about her brother again. It's hard to concentrate on what she's saying when all I can think about is what's going to happen when I open my front door. Fortunately, she's so busy talking, she doesn't notice I'm grinding my teeth.

"Garth gets on the phone with that girl and he doesn't say hardly anything. Then when he hangs up he says, 'It's so great. She's so hot for me and I couldn't care less about her.' That's his idea of the ultimate relationship. And I say, 'Congratulations,' but I mean it sarcastically and he thinks I'm serious. So he goes, 'Thanks, Sis.' Can you believe that?"

"I sort of get it. I mean, he doesn't have to worry about getting hurt. It's pretty intelligent in a warped way."

"What it means is that you end up hanging out with people you have no respect for."

"At least you have a brother. At least you have a whole normal family," I snap at her.

I should tell her about Leon.

I should tell her before we get to my place. She should know what she's getting into. I'll tell her when we pass the last tree on the park path.

I'll tell her when we cross the street. I'll tell her when we turn off. I'll tell her on the doorstep.

I watch our feet walk up the limestone path to the house. I open my mouth to tell her, but it's like I'm standing in front of art class again, not saying the most important thing. I take one last look at Clara's happy face and turn the doorknob.

We're taking off our shoes when Leon comes jogging down the stairs in his green jeans and purple T-shirt. As soon as he sees Clara, he gets this huge honking grin on his face.

"Girlfriends!" he squeals, laying it on thick off the top.

I hate him up and down. Instead of covering it up, he sticks it in your face. I want to plow him down. Why didn't I say anything? Leon swoops down and stands between us.

"So, Gwen, are you going to introduce me?" I swear he's slurring his S's on purpose.

I take a deep breath.

"Leon, this is Clara. Clara, this is Leon, my dad's boyfriend."

Clara sits on my bed holding her knapsack in her lap. She plays with the zipper, flipping the pull up and down and staring at the floor. I close the door and walk around her to the chair at my desk. I clench my hands in my lap and wait for her to say something. Outside, a crow caws, and we both turn our heads to the sound.

"I didn't know. I didn't think..." She lets her voice trail off into the air and rests her chin on her knapsack.

"So?" I say. She turns her head to the side. I stand up and walk in front of her. "Clara, Clara, Clara, my dear girl. You are supposed to say something nice when somebody invites you over to her house. You can say anything you want, but it has to be nice."

"Why didn't you tell me your dad was gay?"

"You know now. You know everything." My voice catches. "You're the first one." But as I say it, I realize it's not true. I told Anisha. My mind whirls back to that day in the park, to me kissing her, to her running away. "You're the first one to meet Leon."

"He seems...so..."

"Gay?" I say the word for her. She nods. "Yeah, I know."

"Is your mother?"

"No. I think they both wanted a family, only it didn't turn out the way they planned. Or at least, it didn't turn out the way my mother planned." The words come out of my mouth and sound true, as if I've known this all along. Clara sits forward on the bed, hugs her knapsack closer and stares at the door.

"She left because of your dad being gay?" she asks.

It's the first time anyone has ever said it out loud. I nod and press my palms against my eyes to make myself disappear. I stand in the middle of my room, pressing the dark against me, not wanting to see what comes next. I hear the creak of my mattress as Clara stands up. I hear her walk across the floor and then the room goes quiet. I wait, holding my breath, but hear no sound. Clara must have gone.

I press harder on my eyes and shake my head.

Someone's hand cups my elbow. I snap my arm away and set my jaw, ready to yell at Leon. But when I blink open, it's Clara. I let loose a wave of tears. I grab Clara's hand and use it to wipe them away. I squeeze it in both my hands. She pries my fingers gently off her hand and wipes the back of her hand on her jeans to dry it off. I laugh.

"So is this what you do here? Sit around and

cry? Don't I get something to eat? At least my family fed you."

I jump up, slam open the bedroom door and
holler, "Leon, tell Dad to pick up some pop on the
way home. Clara's staying for dinner."

⅓

Clara calls home, and Leon gets started on
spaghetti and meatballs. When Dad gets home, he
brings us fizzy pink pop in tall glasses filled with
ice. Clara tries to make a perfectly circular nest out
of one of the beanbag chairs. Once she gets into it,
she can't reach her drink and I have to pass it to
her when she's thirsty so the nest won't get ruined.
Then I make a nest out of my beanbag chair and
neither of us can reach our drinks. We sit crosslegged in our beanbag nests and meditate until we
become serene buddhas who don't need to drink.
Then Dad calls us down to dinner.

I always thought it would be too strange to have
a friend over here with Dad and Leon, but it's
okay. Even with Leon showing off. He slurps a
huge long piece of spaghetti and says "ah" at the
end and you can tell he thinks he's like the clown
at a children's party.

Dad's so happy, I can hardly stand it.

"Stop it," I say to Leon when he slurps yet
another piece of spaghetti.

"Stop what?" he says.

174

"Acting like that."

"How was I acting?"

"Melon," I hiss.

"I have to know how I was acting so that I don't act like that anymore."

Clara starts giggling and then Dad joins in.

"Dad."

I burn him with my eyes and he backs off. He clears his throat. "Gwen told us that your group has won the mural design contest. You must be happy about that, Clara."

"Yeah. It was Gwen's idea and Tony's pictures that won. Tony's the best in our class, except for Gwen, but she gets it from you. I really like your portraits, Mr. Bainbridge." Dad is confused, but I shoot him a look not to say anything. Then Leon pipes up.

"I did those." How many times can you wish a guy dead in one day?

"Oh," says Clara. "I thought you said..."

"That Dad did them?" Everyone holds their forks in the air, waiting. "I lied about the portraits to Anisha and it just sort of grew. I wasn't ready to explain about Leon."

"Why?" says Leon. "What'd I do?"

"Never mind," I growl. "God, what I wouldn't give to live in a normal house, with normal people who were normal."

"Seems pretty normal to me," says Clara, stuffing another meatball in her mouth.

"I like her," says Leon.

"Yes. I do, too," says Dad.

❧

After dinner, we go to my room.

"I have something I want to show you." I make my way to the desk. I get out the postcards and hold them to my chest. "I had this rule about not showing them. I thought I had to keep everything about my parents secret." I pass them to her. She handles them with her fingertips, as if they are precious artifacts. She lays them out on the bed and examines the pictures.

"You can read them if you want," I say. She turns over the first one, the one with the picture of the family camping by the river. I sit on the edge of the bed and watch her read. The black jags of her hair scrape her cheeks as her head moves from side to side.

Her face shows everything. I can almost see the words going into her head. *"I think about you all the time…Oh well. C'est la vie…I can't wait to see your shining face again…time for siesta…when you come to visit…My roommate…Soon angel… I bet grade 7 will be a breeze…mucking it up… Maybe Christmas…"*

When she finishes, she puts them back in order and passes them to me.

"It's too bad," she sighs.

"Well, I do have my dad, and he's good and Leon's not so weird once you get to know him."

"I didn't mean that," says Clara. "I meant it's too bad for your mother that she doesn't know you. I feel sorry for her."

I look down at the postcards in my hands. Then I throw them up to the ceiling and let them float down around us like autumn leaves.

CHAPTER NINETEEN

THE CONSTRUCTION WALL IS UP AND WE'RE outside sketching our superheroes on it. It's cold out. My fingers feel like chalk, but the sun is beaming so bright that it makes the white-washed wall look like it's shining all on its own. I hold my pencil above my head, drag it sideways an inch and stop. In my other hand I'm holding the piece of paper with Tony's Creative Woman on it. I thought I'd think of something better on my own, but it's been hard to shake Creative Woman out of my head. She keeps out-supering my other hero ideas. I press so hard on the pencil that the tip breaks off. I reach in my pocket for my sharpener.

"You're taking up the whole wall. Where are the rest of us supposed to go?" I hear Tim whining around the corner.

"Don't have a weasel," Clara says. I look down the wall at Tony to see if he's listening, but he's smudging a line with his thumb.

"Don't have a weasel? What does that mean?" Tim says. "What are you drawing that you need that much space for?"

"Your oversized head."

Sharpening my pencil, I wander round the corner to take a look. Tim takes me by the shoulders and positions me in front of Clara's spot on the wall.

"Talk to her," he whispers, and walks away.

Clara's drawing is the size of a baby elephant. It's a mountainous lump of...

"I thought you were doing a singer?"

"It's just the outline," she mumbles to the wall.

"The outline of what?"

"Me. The singer."

I stand back to look. Clara's standing in the middle of it with her head against the wall. The outline is bigger than her by about a foot on either side.

I have an idea.

"Put your arms by your side and stand still," I say. Clara shrugs and puts her arms down. I squat down and blow the sharpener shavings off my pencil. I start at her left foot and run the pencil alongside her body. I go up under her arm, around her fingers and over her head. When I'm done, I tell her to step back.

"Look."

Her real outline is about two hundred pounds lighter than the one she drew. She stands there staring.

"Big difference, huh?" I fish her eraser out of her pink pencil case, push it into her hand and leave her there.

I go back and stare at my space on the wall. Soon I can hear Clara humming around the corner. I turn my ear to listen to her and feel a warmth hit my face. It reminds me of a dream I had a long time ago. It was one with my mother in it, where I found her in the park and she stroked my hair as the sun rose.

I lift my pencil to the wall and start to draw. It seems to move almost on its own, like it knows where to go and what to do. I draw hair blown back by the wind. I draw arms opened wide. I draw a long robe with a sun on it. In the middle of the sun I draw an eye.

I line the hem and sleeves of my robe with question marks. Around my waist I draw a chain and on the end of the chain I draw a key. It is the key to everything. Then, because it looks lonely, I draw another key beside it.

I step back and look at my handiwork and notice Tony and Clara standing behind me.

"What is she?" Clara asks.

"She's a see-er and a questioner," I say.

"I've never heard of that," says Tony.

"She is what she is," I say.

"The Quester," says Clara. I nod. I have to put one more thing on my picture. I step forward and draw a line on the side of the robe.

"What's that?" Tony asks.

"A pocket," I say.

"What's in it?"

"It's a secret."

Clara swings her arm over my shoulder. I know she won't ask, but she's the only person I'd tell. Or maybe she's already guessed that deep in the black-velvet pocket of her sunlit robe, the Quester keeps the pieces of the box she once lived in.